P9-DGL-946

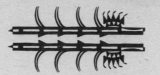

Quest for Courage

Quest for Courage

Stormy Rodolph

Illustrations by
Paulette Livers Lambert

SCHOLASTIC INC.
New York Toronto London Auckland Sydney

For my husband, Ric, with love
and appreciation

No part of this publication may be reproduced in whole or in part, or stored in a retrieval system, or transmitted in any form or by any means, electronic, mechanical, photocopying, recording, or otherwise, without written permission of the publisher. For information regarding permission, write to Roberts Rinehart Publishers, P.O. Box 666, Niwot, CO 80544.

ISBN 0-590-64541-2

Copyright © 1984, 1993 by Stormy Rudolph. All rights reserved. Published by Scholastic Inc., 555 Broadway, New York, NY 10012, by arrangement with Roberts Rinehart Publishers.

12 11 10 9 8 7 6 5 4 3 2 1   5 6 7 8 9/9 0/0

Printed in the U.S.A.   40

First Scholastic printing, October 1995

Contents

The Council for Indian Education Series

The Council for Indian Education is a non-profit organization devoted to teacher training and to the publication of materials to aid in Indian education. All books are selected by an Indian editorial board and are approved for use with Indian children.

The Council for Indian Education Editorial Board

Hap Gilliland, Chairman
Rosalie BearCrane, Crow
Therese WoodenLegs, Northern Cheyenne
Marie Reyhner, Navajo
Juanita Sloss, Blackfeet
Jean BearCrane, Crow
John J. WoodenLegs, Northern Cheyenne
Mary Therese One Bear, Cheyenne
Sally Old Coyote, Crow
Robert La Fountain, Chippewa
Kay Streeter, Sioux
Annette Reid, Tolowa-Yurok
Elaine Allery, Chippewa-Cree
William Spint, Crow
Dolly Plumage, Chippewa-Cree
Joe Cooper, Yurok
Gary Dollarhide, Cherokee
Jerry Cox, Crow
Sharon ManyBeads Bowers, Assiniboine-Haida
Julia Minoz Bradford, Hispanic-Lakota

John Rehner, Indian Education Specialist
Diane Bakun, Teacher, Athapascan Fourth Grade
Willis Buznitz, White River Cheyenne Church
Elizabeth Clark, Secretary of the Board

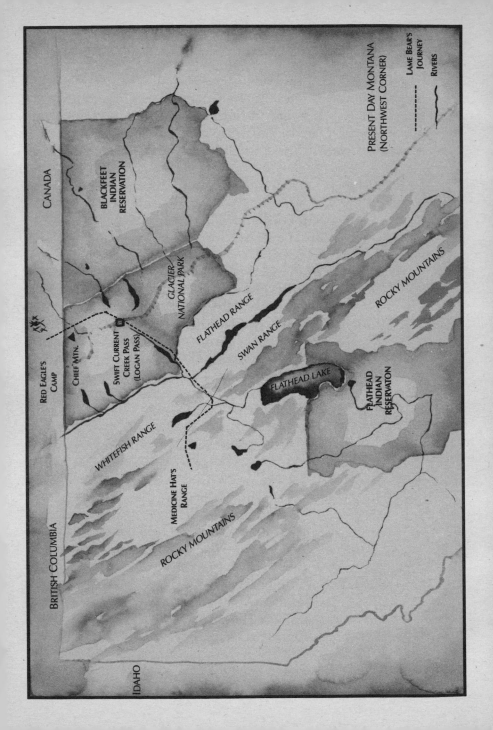

Chapter One

New Hope

 The cougar, wild with pain, crouched on the rocky ledge. Its powerful legs were drawn under, giving it the full benefit of power to leap. The black-tipped tail whipped back and forth.

Lame Bear looked into the cold, yellow eyes, trying to guess when the cougar's charge would come. He reached for his sheathed knife. His soft moccasined feet sought a firmer hold on the rock beneath him. His last arrow was buried deep in the muscles of the cat's tawny shoulder. Now he had it cornered. He braced himself for the attack.

The cougar's scream of rage broke the tension as it sprung . . .

The dull, aching throb of his crippled leg woke Lame Bear out of his dream. The cold bit into him, making him shiver. He waited impatiently while the golden rim of the sun sliced the horizon and rose into the morning sky. It was his duty to go out before dawn and gather the horses closer to the village so they would be easy to catch for the day's hunt. He dreaded the early morning chore.

His body trembled from the pre-dawn chill, and his leg ached from the long walk to the horse herd. Lame Bear hated his leg. The other boys laughed and called him "old woman." The shame was unbearable! A young

Blackfeet's entire childhood was spent developing himself into a strong and courageous warrior. Lame Bear's pain and shame kept him away from the games and hunts of the other boys. He sighed. Was he destined to spend the rest of his life helping the women gather roots, berries, and firewood? The thought sickened him.

His eyes looked sadly toward the horse herd. Today was the big buffalo hunt. For the first time, boys the same age as Lame Bear would demonstrate their horsemanship and hunting skills. They would be able to find glory in the chase. If they were lucky, they might bring down a buffalo calf. This would be the first step leading them from boyhood into manhood. Lame Bear would not be among them.

Lame Bear was not born crippled. Before his leg was broken, he had been very athletic. He seldom lost a footrace, and no one could keep up with him in the water. Now, he missed dancing at the ceremonies most of all. There was nothing to equal the rhythmic beat of the powwow drums, of moccasined feet matching the throb of the drum, beat for beat as each dancer tried to outdance the others. The dance would end with a resounding downbeat, catching all but the best dancers off guard. Lame Bear had never missed a downbeat. These memories stirred his feelings of bitterness. In his heart he knew he could have been a great warrior. Now he had no hope of such honor.

Lame Bear was going into his seventh summer when the accident happened. Six years ago, he and several of his friends were playing war games on their horses. Lame Bear's horse stumbled and fell, landing on his leg. The force of the fall snapped the leg like a dry twig. The medicine man packed it in mud and splint it with sticks, but the bones mended poorly, leaving him with a bad

limp and considerable pain. He was forced to use a tree limb for a crutch. At first, his friends were sympathetic and tried to cheer him up by including him in their play. But as they grew older, they had other things to do, and Lame Bear was left behind, lonely and humiliated.

Sounds coming from the awakening village interrupted Lame Bear's thoughts. He could hear a dog barking, and a horse whinnied in the distance. Smoke began to rise above the flaps of the tipis. The women were stoking the morning fires.

He walked down the hill to his father's lodge. Today he felt especially useless. Lame Bear found his father preparing his weapons. As one of the chiefs of the village, Red Eagle was expected to lead the hunt. Lame Bear avoided his father's eyes when he entered the tipi. Although Red Eagle was never unkind to him, at times he couldn't hide his disappointment. Today was one of those days. He looked up, then quickly dropped his eyes when he saw who it was. It was a hard burden for the chief to bear. Lame Bear was his only son.

As he examined the arrows, Red Eagle spoke to his son. "Did you bring in my red roan horse?"

"Yes, father. He is in the band up on the hill," replied Lame Bear. "Father, I . . ."

Red Eagle put his hand on Lame Bear's shoulder. "I understand your pain. Someday we will ride on a hunt together."

Lame Bear pulled away and ducked out the door. He was ashamed of the tears welling in his eyes. Red Eagle let him go. There was nothing more he could say.

The hunters used two horses on a buffalo hunt. They rode one horse and led their best hunting horse to where the buffalo herd grazed. A good hunting horse was given special care, and was kept tethered near a warrior's tipi.

Fleet Foot was Red Eagle's best hunting horse. It took a horse with exceptional wind, speed, and courage to bring a hunter in for a good kill. Fleet Foot was this kind of horse, and Red Eagle took great pride in him. He had stolen the horse from a Crow chief, making the animal even more valuable among the Blackfeet. Red Eagle smiled to himself every time he recalled the incident. He could imagine the expression on the Crow's face when he stepped out of his lodge and found the severed rope where his horse had been standing.

Now Red Eagle gathered his newest arrows and checked the stone edges for sharpness. Without sharp heads his arrows would not go through the tough hides of the buffalo. He also studied his newest war lance. It took a sharp lance and a brave man to ride close enough to a buffalo to thrust the spear into its heart. Red Eagle hoped he would get a chance to do this during tomorrow's hunt. He wanted to bring honor to his lodge.

Red Eagle walked out into the early morning sunshine. He stretched, facing the warmth of the sun. The powerful muscles across his shoulders and back expanded under his copper skin. A smile came to his ruggedly handsome face. This would be a good day. He turned and looked with admiration at his horse. Fleet Foot was young, proud, and full of spirit. He showed his Spanish mustang ancestry. A powerfully built gray, he had a deep girth and long sloping hip, giving him extra endurance and speed.

The horse snorted softly as Red Eagle approached him. "Easy, young hunter," Red Eagle said. "Today you will make yourself famous among horses." The horse stood hypnotized by the warrior's steady, quiet voice. Then he nuzzled Red Eagle's shoulder playfully.

Dogs barked. Children laughed and ran about. The

women chattered excitedly as the men prepared their horses for the hunt. Finally, the hunters mounted and waited for Red Eagle's signal. Letting out a loud yell, the chief touched heels to his horse and the roan leaped forward. Fleet Foot followed beside, never tightening the lead rope. Dust rose high into the sky as the hunting party raced out of camp, leaving behind the women, the children, and Lame Bear.

The sun went unnoticed in the sky. The singing of the birds went unheard. Lame Bear sat brooding, not taking any interest in the activities of the women preparing to follow the hunting party. Irritated by the laughter of the small children and the busy chatter of the women, he got up and limped out of camp. Bitterness grew in him as he walked across the open meadow. Why did the spirits do this terrible thing to him? What had he done to deserve the suffering and the humiliation?

Lame Bear sat on the bank of the creek with his back to the village. He was so occupied with self-pity that he didn't notice the quiet approach of an old man. When the old man spoke, Lame Bear was so startled that he jumped and slipped, almost falling into the water.

"Why do you sit here like an old woman waiting to die?" the old man asked.

Lame Bear did not feel like talking, but his training would not allow him to be disrespectful to an elder. He fixed his eyes on the ground. "I have no reason to live. The spirits have nothing but evil for me. I might as well be an old woman." As he spoke, tears started, but he could not let the old warrior see them. Lame Bear fought to keep what little pride he had.

The old man stood tall and straight, with a dignity about him that commanded respect. His white hair hung loosely to his shoulders. As he looked at Lame Bear, his wrinkled face softened with compassion. He spoke gently. "My son, why do you let this thing tear at your heart? It is like a sickness that is eating your body. You are strong. Your mind is sharp. Yet you spend your days idle and useless. You are the son of a great chief. Why do you put shame on him?"

These words pierced Lame Bear's heart. He knew there was truth in what the old man said, but he was too consumed with self-pity to admit it. He managed to reply, "It is not my fault I am crippled. I did not ask for this curse. The other boys laugh at me. The spirits have forsaken me. I might as well be dead!"

With kindness and wisdom, the old warrior spoke. "My son, you are young. What do you know of the ways of the spirits? You have not even gone to seek your spirit helper. You are as a summer-born foal that has no idea of the winter which is yet to come. A man does not become a great warrior by sitting in his lodge. He must go out and fight for his honor. The path which your mind is taking is too easy. It will never take you out of your lodge. You must start searching for a better way. It is time for you to go on your vision quest. Come to me when you are ready."

Without another word he turned and walked away, leaving Lame Bear to his thoughts. At first, he resented the old man's words. How could he possibly know what Lame Bear felt? The old man had never felt shame and humiliation. He had been a great warrior for many years, and now in his old age, he had the respect and admiration of the whole village. He could never know!

Lame Bear tried to forget his conversation with the old warrior, but he was unable to push the words from his mind. Could the old man be right? Could a spirit helper help him? A seed of new hope began to take root in Lame Bear's mind.

His thoughts were interrupted by his mother's angry voice. "Are you going to sit there dreaming all day? Hurry. Go get the horses. It is time to follow your father. We have much work to do."

Chapter Two

The Price of Victory

The hunters slowed their horses to a walk once they were out of sight of the village. It would be foolish to tire them early in the day. The horses would need to be strong and fresh when the buffalo were sighted. By mid-morning, the men arrived at the place where the scout had last seen the herd. The grass was short and buffalo chips were plentiful, evidence that a large herd had recently grazed there. The bulls were leading the cows and the calves out on the plains where the grass was lush and more plentiful. Here they would spend the summer, putting on the fat they would need to stay alive through the long winter months.

With increasing excitement the men urged their ponies forward. Red Eagle saw the eagerness in his hunters, and a smile came to his lips. It was a great time to be alive. What more could a man ask for than a fast horse, this beautiful country, a warm lodge, and a son. The smile faded from Red Eagle's face. A man's son would carry on the traditions of the people, bring honor to his father's lodge, and comfort him in his old age. Red Eagle knew he was lucky to have a son. Yet he would never share in his son's achievements as a warrior and a hunter because Lame Bear could never do any of these things. And even though he thought sadly of how the boy must suffer, there were times when Red Eagle was ashamed of Lame Bear's condition.

With a deep sigh, Red Eagle reached over to stroke the satin neck of the gray stallion. "Fleet Foot, you have become like a son to me. It is only through you that I can gain victory." The horse's ears twitched back and forth as he listened to the gentle voice. There was a strong bond of friendship between them.

By noon the hunters were getting close to their prey. The horses became excited when they caught the rank scent of the buffalo. They began prancing sideways, pulling against the restraining rawhide on their mouths. The men could tell the herd was near by the strong musk odor.

Red Eagle appointed two men to scout the exact position of the herd. The scouts left the camp on foot, taking with them two wolf skins. They climbed a small knoll which kept them out of the buffalo's sight. Near the top, they got down on their hands and knees and pulled the wolf skins over their heads and shoulders. Then they crawled over the crest of the hill toward the buffalo herd.

The nearest animals raised their heads in mild curiosity at the approach of the disguised scouts. Wolves were a common sight and aroused no fear in the buffalo. Only the sick, the old, and the very young had to fear the ripping teeth of the wolves. Downwind, the scouts approached to within a stone's throw of the herd. They saw everything they needed to know.

On hearing the scout's report, the hunters mounted their hunting horses. Red Eagle briefly mapped out their approach to the buffalo. The riders would fan out and move in from the north, forcing the herd to run in a southerly direction. Once the buffalo were in full stam-

pede, the riders could flank them, seeking out the choicest kills.

The hunters topped the crest of the hill and kicked their ponies into a run. Each man yelled at the top of his lungs. The buffalo stood momentarily stunned by the sight and sound of the charging hunters. Then, like an avalanche gathering momentum, the huge herd started moving. Within seconds they were in full stampede.

Each hunter singled out an animal for his first kill, and guided his horse toward it. During the chase, Red Eagle killed several choice cows. Fleet Foot was still running strong beneath him when he spotted one of the "yellow ones." This female had never lost her yellow baby color, making her hide very valuable. Red Eagle saw his chance for a great victory in this animal. Fleet Foot, sensing Red Eagle's excitement, moved eagerly in on the buffalo. The cow tried to outrun the horse. Her mouth frothed. Her nostrils dilated to a blood red and her eyes rimmed white with terror. Fleet Foot moved Red Eagle into a good killing position. Grabbing his lance in both hands, Red Eagle leaned over to make the killing thrust.

Red Eagle put all of his strength behind his thrust. The cow bellowed in pain, maddened by the smell of her own blood. Blood gushed from her mouth and nostrils. She ran a few more yards until she finally went to her knees. A great shudder ran through her and she lay still.

With the last reflex of the buffalo's body, Red Eagle gave a sigh of relief. He pulled his blowing horse to a stop. Sweat dripped from Fleet Foot's heaving flanks and his legs trembled. Red Eagle turned to admire his kill, and did not see the other wounded buffalo. The cow was crazy with pain. In the blur of motion around her, the sudden stillness of the horse and rider caught her attention. She let out a bellow and charged. Fleet Foot saw her coming, but in his exhaustion, turned too slowly. The mammoth head of the cow hit Fleet Foot in the side, throwing the horse off his feet. The impact threw Red Eagle from his mount. He lay stunned and helpless. His arrows were lost and his only lance was embedded in the body of the dead cow.

One of the hunters, seeing Red Eagle's plight, charged his horse through the swirling mass of animals. A well-aimed arrow brought the cow to her knees. The gored stallion lay shivering and groaning. The hunter took his knife and mercifully cut the throat of the suffering horse. Fleet Foot's spirit departed. The hunter cut off a lock of his mane and put it in his medicine pouch. Red Eagle slowly walked over to his dead friend and did the same thing. This was the price of victory. It left only empti-ness in Red Eagle's heart.

Chapter Three

The Decision

 Lame Bear was eager to obey his mother. A new sense of anticipation filled him. Something was going to happen. He could feel it. It was like waking up after being asleep for a long time.

His mother was surprised by his instant obedience. Usually she had to speak to him several times before he would do what she asked. Now, he was limping without complaint, joining the other boys to gather the horses needed for the day's work—a long, hard day of skinning buffalo. As she watched him go, she wondered what he had been thinking about when she scolded him. It had been a long time since she had seen him smile like he was now.

Lame Bear looked over the horse herd. He located his pinto mare and the old buckskin his mother used to pull their pole and rawhide travois. A soft whistle brought the pinto mare to him, but the buckskin was less willing to be caught. He played cat and mouse, weaving in and out among the other horses, just out of Lame Bear's reach. Lame Bear laughingly scolded the old horse. "You old fox, you know today you must work. Why do you play games? A horse your age should know better," he said.

When he returned with the two horses, his mother scolded him for taking so long, but he knew she was too excited to be serious. It was not long before the travois

14

was in place behind the buckskin. Lame Bear mounted the pinto, and he and his mother headed out of camp in the direction of the hunters. Soon the other women and children were following behind them.

He urged his mare into a trot. He wanted to be the first one to find the buffalo kills. There was no shade from the mid-afternoon sun on the plains so it was important for the group to find the meat quickly. If the carcasses lay too long in the sun, they would spoil.

Lame Bear stopped at the top of the knoll they were climbing, thrilled by the sight before him. The plains were dotted with bodies of dead buffalo. His first impulse was to yell for joy and run his mare off the hill, but he was afraid the hunters would think him foolish if they saw him. He walked the mare calmly down the slope. His job was to find the first buffalo his father had killed. Each warrior had his own mark on his weapons. This settled the ownership of the kill. If two different arrows were found in the body, the carcass was shared by both families.

Among the many dead animals, Lame Bear finally found Red Eagle's arrow. He dismounted and quickly went to work on the carcass. First, he skinned the buffalo, his sharp knife slashing the membrane that held the hide to the meat. Then he gutted the animal, being careful not to puncture any organs. Every part of the buffalo would be used. Nothing was wasted. When the carcass was cut into smaller pieces, the meat would be wrapped in the hide so it could be hauled more easily on the travois.

Lame Bear enjoyed his work, but he was also impatient to see the hunters. Chills always went down his spine when he listened to their stories about the hunt. He thrilled to see them riding into the village, singing victory songs and showing off their horsemanship. The celebration that followed was always an exciting time of feasting, dancing and storytelling. But when the boys his own age would get up to tell their own stories of victory, Lame Bear would leave the gathering and brood about his failings. If only someday he could be telling such stories about himself!

He stood up from skinning the buffalo and walked toward his mare. Her alert pose stopped him short. She was staring intently at something out on the prairie. Fearing it might be an enemy, he whistled the mare over to him. He quickly hid her in a hollow behind a low hill, then crawled on his belly to the top of the hill and peeked over. His vision blurred for a few seconds because of the shimmering heat waves. As his eyes began to focus, he could make out the shapes of horses and riders. They were in a circle around something, but he could not tell what it was. The women and other children were now busy butchering the buffalo kills. They would never miss him. He mounted his mare, and rode out of the hollow toward the strange gathering on the plains.

News of Red Eagle's plight spread rapidly through the hunting party. Every man headed his horse toward the scene of the struggle. Two Feathers had been the first hunter to arrive. It was he who killed the enraged cow and mercifully ended Fleet Foot's suffering. The other hunters, seeing that nothing could be done, gathered in respectful silence around the dead horse. Generally not much attention was paid to the death of a horse. But Fleet Foot was their chief's horse, and he had been coveted by each one of them.

No man in the Blackfeet nation had ever ridden him except Red Eagle. Together they had won many honors for the tribe. Today had been no exception. Many of the warriors felt Fleet Foot had special spirit powers. Several

of them came forward and cut off pieces of the stallion's mane to put in their medicine pouches. They would then carry these powers with them always.

Red Eagle was in shock, making it hard for him to comprehend Fleet Foot's death. It was like a horrible dream and he could not wake up. He fingered the coarse, black mane he held between his fingers. Never again would it be lifted off the sleek, gray neck by the wind. Red Eagle closed his eyes, seeing in his mind the grace and speed of the gray stallion. It was no good! He must try to forget. Looking up, he recognized Lame Bear's pinto mare coming toward him. What was the boy doing here? Was it really so late in the day? He could not bear the thought of seeing his son's face. Lame Bear had not yet seen Fleet Foot.

Lame Bear approached the distant horsemen with caution. As he neared the group he began to recognize the hunting party. Some great event must have taken place for the riders to be gathered that way. He kicked his mare into a lope. The first thing he noticed was the "yellow one" with the shaft of his father's spear sticking out of it. The color of the cow's shaggy hair made his heart race. What a victory for Red Eagle and Fleet Foot! His eyes searched for his father and the gray stallion. He saw his father, but what was he doing on the ground? Where was Fleet Foot? Then he saw him, and a wave of nausea washed over Lame Bear at the terrible sight.

That bloody mess of horse flesh was not Fleet Foot. It couldn't be! Quickly he searched his father's face for the answer. Red Eagle's expression spoke louder than words. Hot tears welled in Lame Bear's eyes. He turned his mare away, and then he cried. He cried for Fleet Foot, but most of all, he cried for his father.

The little pinto mare walked on into the evening, her

rider unaware of where she was going. Only when she came to a stream and stopped to drink did Lame Bear react. He slid from her back and buried his face in the sparkling cold water. Its icy fingers worked on his brain and broke it loose from its stupor. When Lame Bear climbed back on his mare he was changed. With definite purpose, he turned her back toward their village. In the morning, he would go to see the old warrior, Fine Bull.

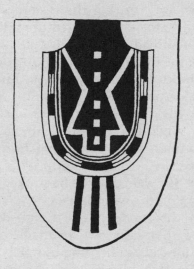

Chapter Four

The Quest

Dawn was turning the eastern sky a pale rose when Lame Bear entered the village. The cold night air had left his body stiff and sore. He had spent most of the night riding, thinking of the old man's words. He guided his mare directly to Fine Bull's lodge near the outside perimeter of the camp. No one noticed his return. At the lodge entrance he slid slowly from the mare's back. When his feet struck the ground, a sharp pain shot through his leg, causing him to groan. He limped to the mare's head and slipped the guide rope out of her mouth. She waited while he stroked her neck, then trotted out to join the other horses.

Lame Bear was suddenly filled with doubts. He was afraid Fine Bull might not be there, or might have changed his mind about helping him. He was also afraid his gift of a small rabbit would not be enough. But then the memory of Fleet Foot's mutilated body gave him new courage. He pushed the door flap aside and quickly entered the lodge. He stood still a moment, letting his eyes get accustomed to the darkness.

"My son, what took you so long?" It was the voice of Fine Bull.

"How did you know it was me?" Lame Bear asked.

"I heard the approaching steps of your horse and when you dismounted, your pain. But what puzzles me is why you waited so long to enter my lodge." The old man leaned back against his sleeping mat and studied Lame Bear's face. Fine Bull heard of Red Eagle's tragedy when runners brought back the news to the village. He suspected this was why Lame Bear had come to him so suddenly, but he did not ask.

Lame Bear stood silent, not knowing what to say. He did not want to tell Fine Bull what had happened to his father. Pity was the last thing he wanted. "I have come to seek your help. You spoke of my need to find a spirit helper. I have come. I am ready." Then he added, "When can we start?"

"When do you want to start?" asked Fine Bull.

"Now," said Lame Bear.

"As you wish." Fine Bull rose slowly to his feet. "Come with me."

The old man quickly gathered the things he would need and placed them in a bundle. He motioned Lame Bear to follow, and they slipped quietly out of the lodge. The village was not yet awake. The hunters and their families were exhausted from their long day and late return the evening before, and the feasting and storytelling that lasted most of the night.

Fine Bull stopped at another tipi not far from his own. Lame Bear stayed outside, but he could hear the low sound of two men talking. Fine Bull soon emerged from the tipi, followed by another old man. This man was to help Fine Bull and Lame Bear with the purification ritual.

Together, they headed in the direction of the mountains. The snowcapped peaks showed pink in the dawn. Lame Bear grew faint as he faced them. Never before had his leg felt so weak. He wanted desperately to turn and run to the warmth and the security of his father's lodge.

He was sure he would die up there in the mountains. He had heard stories of young boys who had gone on their vision quests and never returned. They had been strong and healthy with two good legs. As these thoughts raced through Lame Bear's mind, Fine Bull's steady pace took them deeper and deeper into the high country.

Lame Bear began to notice his surroundings. He had never been in such country, and the beauty awed him. Above him, the peaks looked as if they had been carved with a sharp knife. Deep lakes fed by melting glaciers gleamed a bright, turquoise blue in the sun. He had heard others tell stories about these lakes and mountains, but they had not done justice to the view before him.

They stopped in a small, grassy clearing, facing a grove of aspens and a clear, mountain spring. The pungent smell of pines hung heavy in the hot air. Lame Bear closed his eyes and breathed in deeply, as the warmth of the sun eased his aching muscles.

Fine Bull's voice broke the silence. "It is time for you to build the sweat lodge. We will prepare the fire."

Lame Bear quickly gathered the saplings he needed to build his sweat lodge. He placed one end of each stick in the ground, bent them into a graceful arc, and then secured the other ends in the ground. Then he covered this framework completely with hides. A small entrance facing the east was left open until the purification was to take place.

When Lame Bear was finished, he sat down and studied the mountains until he saw one peak that towered above the others. Its summit reached beyond the limits of his mind. He asked Fine Bull the name of the mountain.

Fine Bull turned to look where Lame Bear pointed. His old eyes squinted against the glare of the sun. "That is Thunder Mountain, my son."

Lame Bear had heard many legends about Thunder Mountain. The Blackfeet believed the mountain had great spirit powers. Sometimes it spoke in a great thundering voice, and nobody went near it at that time. The mountain did most of its thundering in the Spring, when huge chunks of ice would break off of the glacier and fall into the lake below.

Suddenly, Lame Bear understood, and panic seized him. This was where Fine Bull was going to send him on his cry for power! The idea of facing the mountain alone terrified him. He thought of sneaking away, but it was too late. Fine Bull was calling him. "Come, it is time to enter the sweat lodge."

Fine Bull went into the sweat lodge first. Inside, he purified himself with sweet grass. He then lit the sacred pipe and offered it in prayer to all of the Earth Powers. When he finished his prayers, he called Lame Bear.

"My son, you may come into the lodge now," the old man said.

Wearing only his breechcloth, Lame Bear entered the sweat lodge. Without speaking, he sat down cross-legged beside Fine Bull. The old warrior said more prayers, asking the spirits to be merciful to Lame Bear as he cried for power. He then gave the pipe to Lame Bear, who offered it to the powers. Fine Bull said more prayers. He asked for Lame Bear's protection and success. The helper outside brought in the hot rocks and a bladder filled with water. The rocks sizzled and spit as he poured the cold water over them. Steam began to fill the lodge as the helper left and closed the entrance. Lame Bear and Fine Bull were engulfed in a darkness so thick they could feel it pressing in on them.

Time stood still for Lame Bear as sweat ran down his body, cleansing him of all impurities. The helper came into the lodge three more times with hot rocks and water. Each time he raised the entrance flap, the bright light stabbed Lame Bear's eyes.

The darkness and the steam continued to press in on Lame Bear. He felt weak and breathless. He wanted to shout, to yell, anything to break the oppressive silence, but no sound would come from his throat. Just when he thought he could stand no more, Fine Bull spoke. "It is time to go."

The outside flap was thrown open. Lame Bear raised his arm to shield his eyes. Weakly, he crawled through the entrance on his hands and knees and out into the sunshine. His skin was hot and sweaty, but the gentle breeze cooled and caressed his body, making him feel totally relaxed.

Again, Fine Bull spoke. "It is time for us to go. The sun is low in the sky and we have far to travel. You must go to Thunder Mountain and climb as high as you can. When you can go no further, find a level place where you can make your cry for power. You may take no food, water, or weapons. May the spirits hear your cry for power."

Lame Bear said nothing. He stood before the old man, wearing only his breech cloth. He shivered, and Fine Bull took a buffalo robe and draped it over Lame Bear's head and around his shoulders. The old warrior then handed Lame Bear a leather pouch filled with sweetgrass and polished elk teeth, and a prayer fan of eagle feathers to carry before him as he made prayer offerings to the Earth Powers. Fine Bull wrapped himself in his own robe, and headed in the direction of Thunder Mountain. Lame Bear followed.

The shadows grew long, urging the travelers to get as near to the base of the mountains as they could before darkness overtook them. For the first time that day, Lame Bear became painfully aware of how tired he was. His leg had gone to sleep in the sweat lodge, and now it prickled and throbbed. With each step he felt it would collapse under him.

The darkness sharpened Lame Bear's awareness to a keen edge. He did not miss a sound or a movement. Its faint light shimmered through the pine trees. In the distance, a lone coyote howled. Soon it was joined by other coyotes. The night air filled with their spine-tingling chorus. A great horned owl swooped noiselessly out of the trees in search of prey.

When they came to a small spring, the old man dropped down on his stomach and drank deeply. Lame Bear followed his example. He had been allowed to drink before he entered the sweat lodge. Now, he could not drink until after sunset each day. After that, food was forbidden him until his return from Thunder Mountain. He was determined to ignore his growling stomach. He found a soft place under some pine trees, lay down and pulled the buffalo robe tightly around himself. Exhaustion overcame him and he slipped into a deep slumber.

Fine Bull woke up as soon as the eastern sky began to grow light. He walked over to Lame Bear and gently touched the boy's shoulder. "Come. Wake up. It is time for you to go."

Lame Bear looked bewildered. He rubbed his sleep-filled eyes and squinted at Fine Bull. "What is wrong? What is it?"

As soon as he spoke, he became keenly aware of his sore body and the sharp pangs of hunger gnawing at his stomach. Now he remembered! He hated to crawl out from under his robe, but he knew he would need an early start. Today's journey would be long and difficult.

Fine Bull spoke. "I can go no further with you. I must leave. May the spirits hear your cry for power."

Lame Bear opened his mouth to speak. "But I . . ."

Fine Bull had already turned away and was walking back down the trail. Lame Bear hesitated a moment, then went to the spring. He splashed the icy water on his face and body, bringing all of his senses acutely alive. With his eyes on Thunder Mountain, he rolled up his robe and pouch and started on his journey. The trail was still fairly easy, and he rejoiced in the beauty of the day. The first rays of the morning sun began to warm his back, taking away some of the early morning chill. The forest came alive with the singing of birds. Dew sparkled on the blades of grass and on the tips of the pine needles. As he walked through this enchanted forest he was filled with a profound appreciation of life. His limp went unnoticed, and his pain and sorrow were temporarily forgotten.

The sun rose higher in the sky. Lame Bear found the trail becoming increasingly more difficult. It was not long before the forest lost its enchantment. He focused all of his attention on where he was walking. The trail rose sharply and fallen timber hindered his progress.

Lame Bear stopped often, his chest heaving from shortness of breath. He was beginning to feel the effects of no food and the high altitude. His stomach ached dully and his mouth felt sandy dry. He sat down on a log and looked at his crippled leg. It was noticeably smaller than his other leg, and his muscles were twitching spasmodically. It reminded him of a rabbit he had once killed. Even after it was dead, its muscles had twitched and jumped just like the ones in his leg were doing now. The longer Lame Bear looked at his leg the more it seemed not to be a part of him, as if he could just pick it up and throw it away. With a sigh, he got up from the log and headed up the trail.

By mid-afternoon the heat became unbearable. Lame Bear picked up a pebble and put it in his mouth. His saliva started working and temporarily relieved the dryness. His head spun. He sat down in the shade of a tree and gratefully leaned back against the trunk. He wondered if he would ever reach Thunder Mountain, and if it was worth trying. His body felt staked to the earth. He had no will to rise. Discouraged and exhausted, his thoughts turned to venison steaks and cold mountain streams.

Suddenly the silence was shattered by a raucous, scolding squawk. Lame Bear looked up and saw a fat gray bird sitting on a branch not far above his head. The bird was large, its gray feathers accented by black-and-white markings. Its bright, black eyes shone inquisitively. It was noted for its boldness and habit of carrying things away from camp sites.

Lame Bear was surprised by the bird's arrival. His thoughts had been far away. "Hello, little brother. What are you doing here?"

The bird squawked and chattered, ruffling its feathers.

"Ah, I see. You wonder the same about me. I am not sure, little brother. Maybe the Trickster is playing a joke on me," said Lame Bear.

The bird jumped from limb to limb, stopping now and then to preen its feathers. Lame Bear enjoyed the bird's company and had forgotten his discomfort for the moment. With a loud squawk, the bird left its tree and flew up the trail. Lame Bear could hear it chattering in the trees up ahead. It seemed to call to him, encouraging him to follow. Lame Bear smiled and got to his feet. "All right, little brother, you win. I am coming," he said.

For two hours the bird kept to the trail. Sometimes it would stay near Lame Bear, then it would fly far ahead. But it always returned to cheer him on his way. Lame Bear knew that without the bird's company he would not be able to keep going.

At the top of a steep rise, the trail took a sudden dip downward. The trees began to thin out as the trail progressed down the hill. The frantic chattering of the bird drew Lame Bear's attention from the path. He walked over to where the bird was perched in a juniper tree and did not immediately see the view before him. When he finally lowered his gaze, he drew in his breath sharply. Never in his life had he seen anything like what lay before him now.

Thunder Mountain rose majestically to the sky. Every inch of its surface was marked by sharp crags and crevices and steep dropoffs. Halfway down the face of the mountain was a huge glacial field, one of the last remnants of the Ice Age. Small streams trickled out from under the ice into the turquoise lake at its base. Its surface shimmered in the afternoon sun. The grey bird ceased its idle chatter. Lame Bear stood still. His heart swelled and his eyes brimmed with tears. The power of the mountain filled him until everything else was pushed out.

Finally, Lame Bear came out of the spell and began to work his way around the lake. After much scouting and detouring, he came to the headwaters of the lake at the base of the mountain. As he studied the trail he realized he could not get above the glacial field. But he would set out to get as close to the ice pack as possible. The climb was steep and he did much of it on his hands and knees. He did not notice the bleeding cuts. All of his movements were mechanical now. He was obsessed with only one thought: to keep climbing until he could go no further.

The last rays of the sun were swiftly disappearing when Lame Bear finally pulled himself up on a ledge. It was six feet long and three feet deep. It was not much, but it was as far as he could go. A cold wind blew down off the glacier, chilling him to the bone.

Lame Bear quickly made an altar. He placed his offerings and his pipe on the ledge. He said prayers to all of the great powers, asking them to grant his success as he cried for power. Then, he pulled his buffalo robe tightly around himself and stood with his back against the rock wall. Darkness settled over him, making him one with the mountain and the night.

Chapter Five

The Vision

Lame Bear stayed on the ledge for three days and three nights. He had lost all sense of time.

He spent his days praying to the Earth Powers, asking them to send him a spirit helper. At night, he slept by his altar with his feet pointing to the east.

He was no longer aware that his body was numb from cold, hunger, and dehydration. Now his mind was in a much greater state of anguish than his body. The vision had not come. The spirits must be turning their backs on him because he was crippled. Lame Bear ground his teeth and cursed his leg, but his mind was made up. He would stay on the ledge until he died, if that was what the spirits wanted.

Storm clouds gathered in the late afternoon of the fourth day. Big, white, thunderheads loomed over Thunder Mountain. The soft, whispering pines began to roar as the storm whipped through them. Darkness came early to the ledge, and with it came a driving rain. Lightning flashed and thunder echoed and re-echoed off the rock walls. Lame Bear sat down against the cliff. Neither his body nor his mind registered the rain that pelted him. The night and the storm seemed endless.

With the dim light of dawn, the mountains were clothed in heavy fog. The mist was so thick Lame Bear could taste it on his parched lips. It gave a cool, tingling sensation to his swollen, burning tongue. He leaned his head back against the rock and longed for release from his ordeal.

A distant rhythmic tattoo caught Lame Bear's attention. He shook his head to clear the sound from his ears, but it was still there, growing louder. All of Lame Bear's senses concentrated on the beat. It was a galloping horse! His father must have come looking for him. Fine Bull had betrayed his confidence! No matter. He would not go back, not even with his father. Whoever it was, he was riding recklessly. The trail was much too treacherous for anything but walking, even on a clear day.

While Lame Bear waited to see who was coming up the trail, he was surrounded by a brilliant, white light. He threw up his arm to shield his eyes and trembled in bewilderment. From somewhere within the light, a deep voice spoke to him. "Lame Bear, do not be afraid. I have brought your spirit helper. You may look at me now."

Lame Bear slowly dropped his arm. Standing before him in midair was the most magnificent warrior he had ever seen. The man was dressed in full ceremonial costume of white buckskin. The designs made by the delicately colored quills stood out against the white background like the first flowers of spring stand out on a snow-covered hillside. His black hair hung over his shoulders, shining like the wing feathers of the raven.

Lame Bear tried to speak, but could not. He took up his pipe and touched it to his lips. He then offered it to the spirit before him. After sharing Lame Bear's pipe, the warrior and the light disappeared as suddenly as they had come. Again there was the sound of hoofbeats, and a shrill neigh pierced the air. It was a familiar call, yet something about it sent a chill down Lame Bear's spine. He knew that horse! Then he saw it in front of him, the

black mane whipping off the silver neck in the wind. Lame Bear gasped. Fleet Foot! He closed his eyes and then opened them quickly. The horse was still there. Lame Bear's heart pounded in his chest and his breath came in short gasps.

The spirit horse came near him. The expression on the animal's face was almost human. It spoke quietly. "Do not be afraid. It is I, Fleet Foot. The Earth Powers have sent me to be your spirit helper. I have a message for you. Listen carefully, because I can tell you this only once. My death was no accident. It was necessary so I could help you. It was a horse that brought you the shame of your crippled leg. It will be a horse that will raise you up in honor. On the back of a fine horse your bad leg will mean nothing. You will need a powerful horse, one that is swift and full of courage. I cannot tell you what this horse looks like. You must search for him, and when you find him you will know him as your own. The Earth Powers are giving you the gift of the horseman. With this gift and my help, you will be able to handle any horse. I must go now. If you need my help, call out to me and I will be with you." With a toss of his head, Fleet Foot wheeled and galloped into the mist.

For a long time, Lame Bear could not move. He was having doubts about the reality of his vision when he noticed a strange object on the ledge. He reached down and picked up the lock of black horsehair. Many times he had run his fingers through this same black mane. It belonged to Fleet Foot.

Lame Bear took the medicine pouch from around his neck and carefully placed the horsehair in it. Then he picked up his buffalo robe and eased himself off the ledge. Almost blindly, he stumbled down the trail. He walked and walked until he fell to the ground near a bubbling mountain spring. He dragged himself forward until his face reached the water. He touched the cold water to his dry, cracked lips, and over his face. He drank in small sips from his cupped hands, but the shock of the water cramped his stomach, and he doubled over in pain.

Most of the morning Lame Bear rested by the spring, drinking small amounts until it no longer hurt. The sun finally burned its way through the fog and warmed his aching body. He lay back in the cool grass and fell asleep. Lame Bear slept until dawn of the next day. When he woke, the sun was just rising over the tops of the mountains. The sharp pain in his stomach reminded him that he must get food today, or he would never make it back to camp. He refreshed himself at the spring, then headed for the forest in search of food. His hunger was soon relieved by the edible roots he found there.

Lame Bear reflected on what had happened to him. It all seemed unreal. He had to take the horsehair from his medicine pouch to convince himself that he had really had a vision. Holding the hair in his hand, he squeezed it tightly. A big smile spread across his face. He let out a yell and ran down the trail. He could hardly wait to find Fine Bull. He would tell him the vision had come, and he would ask the old man's advice about what he should do next.

Lame Bear was so excited he did not realize he was running on his bad leg. The past days of strenuous exercise had strengthened him. Since his accident it had been easier to make excuses than to work to rise above his handicap. Now, events had forced him to look outside himself. Self-pity had its final death struggle within his heart.

By mid-afternoon, Lame Bear reached the open meadow where he had been purified. It seemed as if years had passed since that day. His excitement rose. He knew that by nightfall he would be in the lodge of Fine Bull. But he would not return to his father's lodge until he could bring honor and victory with him.

As he hurried down the trail, the words of Fleet Foot echoed in his mind. How was he going to find the horse he needed? He had never captured and tamed a wild one. He had no experience. He did not even know where to begin to look for such a horse. This horse must be very special, not just any horse that any brave might own. Lame Bear had heard stories about a great horse that roamed to the south, but surely those were just stories. He knew of no horse that could live up to the descriptions he had heard. His only hope was that Fine Bull would know what to do.

Something in the air made Lame Bear stop. He inhaled deeply. It was the smell of smoke, campfire smoke! He stepped out of the trees and into the open. His first impulse was to run down the hill, giving his loudest victory yell, but he stopped himself. He must go to Fine Bull's lodge unseen. He found shelter in some bushes and sat down to wait for the protective cover of darkness. He had to make sure not even a dog would sense his approach to the camp.

Thoughts of wild horses made the time go quickly. There was no moon. The darkness was complete. Lame Bear looked up into the star-filled heavens and sighed. It was time to go. Carefully, he worked his way down the hill, taking advantage of cover whenever he could. Once he came too close to one of the warrior society guards who dept watch over the camp at night. He froze in his tracks, praying the warrior would not see him. A disturbance in the horse herd finally drew the man away, allowing him to slip through the circle of guards.

At the edge of the camp Lame Bear peered through the darkness until he located Fine Bull's tipi. Then he moved quickly. This time he did not hesitate outside the entrance, but slid under the flap in a flash. The tipi was filled with a soft glow from the dying campfire.

"Welcome back, my son." It was the voice of the old man.

It was not easy to sneak up on him. He seemed to know everything. He did not miss a sound. Lame Bear smiled and his heart swelled with love for the old man.

Fine Bull took an ember from the coals and lit his pipe. "Sit down and tell me of your adventure."

He put the pipe to his lips and drew deeply on the sweet smoke. Then he handed the pipe to Lame Bear. He took a short puff, still not used to the burning sensation of the smoke entering his lungs. He coughed once, but tried again before handing the pipe back to Fine Bull. There was a smile of approval on the old warrior's lips. Lame Bear looked at him, not sure where to begin his story. He cleared his throat nervously.

"The journey to Thunder Mountain was long and hard. Near the end I wanted to give up. I sat down under a tree and felt as if I would never rise again. Then a gray bird came and kept me company. It made me feel much better. I was able to continue my journey to the mountain. The bird stayed with me the whole time. Thunder Mountain was beautiful. I did not know anything on earth could be so wonderful. I went around the lake and did as you told me. I climbed as high as I could until I reached a ledge, and there I stopped to wait for my vision. I do not remember much after that except there was a terrible storm. The next morning the fog was so heavy I could barely see. Then . . . "

"Yes, my son, go on. What happened then?" the old man asked.

Lame Bear blushed. He was afraid Fine Bull would laugh at what he had seen. Then he remembered the hair in his medicine pouch and hurried on with his story. "I heard the sound of a horse running and a neigh. The sky was filled with a light brighter than the sun, and a great warrior appeared, telling me not to be afraid. Then I saw a swift hunting horse coming to me out of the fog. He told me he was my spirit helper, and he had a message for me from the Earth Powers. I am to find and capture a horse that will bring me honor and glory. My spirit helper said this horse will help me to become a great warrior among my people."

Lame Bear stopped. He was breathing hard. He reached in his medicine pouch and brought out the hair, and handed it to Fine Bull. The old man studied the hair carefully. He put it to his nose and smelled it. He was satisfied. Custom did not allow either he or Lame Bear to mention the spirit helper's name out loud, but he knew who it was and it made him happy.

"My son, this is good. The Earth Powers are wise. They sent the gray bird to give you courage and to comfort you in your loneliness. Without the bird you may never have reached Thunder Mountain. Your vision is good. Now you must carry out the swift one's message. Tomorrow you must prepare to go in search of the great horse he told you about."

Fine Bull continued. "There is one horse," he said. "You have heard stories of him. His range is to the south, in the land of the Flatheads. I saw him only once, and that was during his first summer. He is a Medicine Hat, a sacred horse among the people. The dark-haired shield on his chest will protect his rider from the weapons of the enemy. The dark hair over his ears and the top of his head is like a war bonnet, making him chief over all horses. The one who rides such a horse will never be wounded in battle, and will be respected by all men."

The old man leaned forward, his voice almost a whisper. "To find this horse will be difficult and dangerous. If the Flatheads catch you, they will kill you. Capturing the stallion will be no easy task, either. Many great warriors have tried. Of course, there are many fine horses in this country. It would not be so dangerous for you to capture one of them."

"No. I must have the Medicine Hat," replied Lame Bear. "No other horse will do. I will get him or die trying."

Fine Bull got up to put more wood on the fire. "It is good. You will spend the night with me, and tomorrow we will prepare you for your journey. First you must eat."

Lame Bear ate until his stomach bulged. Fine Bull grunted his satisfaction and lay down to sleep. Lame Bear lay down too, but sleep would not come to him. Somewhere to the south, in the land of the Flatheads, a young stallion waited.

Chapter Six

All for a Horse

 "Wake up. It is time to go. The camp will be stirring soon. Hurry!" Fine Bull's voice was urgent.

Lame Bear was in a deep sleep. He became vaguely aware of someone touching him and talking to him. He tried to shut out the voice but it persisted. He moaned and pulled his buffalo robe up over his head. Suddenly, the robe was whipped from his body, and the cold morning air brought him abruptly out of his dreams.

"What is it? What has happened?" he asked. Then he remembered. His aching, tired body, and the sight of Fine Bull brought it all back to him. He had just returned and now he must leave again. He groaned softly.

Fine Bull looked at Lame Bear with understanding and compassion. "You are tired, but you cannot stay here. Someone will see you and tell your father. I will take you to a safe place where you can rest before your long journey. Come, we must get our horses and go."

Fine Bull and Lame Bear walked out to the horse herd. The old warrior had told the warrior society of the boy's need for secrecy. They agreed to keep his trust. Nobody said a word as they passed through the circle of camp guards.

Lame Bear started to whistle for his pinto mare, but Fine Bull stopped him. "No, you must take one of my horses. Your pony would be missed and someone would start looking for you. There is my herd, over there." They walked quietly among the grazing horses. "You should take a mare," said Fine Bull. "She will help you win the big one's heart."

In the dim, pre-dawn light it was difficult to distinguish individual horses. Finally, Fine Bull spotted the horse he wanted. She was nibbling daintily on the dew-covered grass, not really hungry, just passing time until she could bask in the rays of the early morning sun. Fine Bull caught the mare and another horse for himself. He led them quietly away from the herd. They gathered Lame Bear's belongings and left camp, heading south.

After riding in silence for some time, Fine Bull spoke. "You have far to travel into unfamiliar country. Go south, cross the Belly River, and keep going until you reach Chief Mountain. You will know it by its steep sides and flat top. Keep Chief Mountain on your right and ride until you come to Swift Current Creek. Follow the creek to its headwaters. There you will see the pass through the mountains that will take you to the land of the Flatheads. The horse herd you are looking for ranges in the upper end of the Flathead Valley.

Lame Bear rode quietly beside the old man. He ran the words over and over in his mind. It would be time wasted to get lost, and he would be short on time as it was. He had to get back through the pass before the fall snows closed it. This would give him three moons at the most. Lame Bear sighed. The task before him seemed impossible, yet he had no choice but to keep going.

It was mid-morning when Fine Bull headed his horse into an aspen grove. He dismounted at the edge of a small, grassy, glade and turned his horse loose to graze. After unpacking his provisions, Lame Bear did the same.

"We will stop here all day," Fine Bull said. "You need to let your body and mind rest. Tonight we will talk." The old man turned and walked away in search of a comfortable place to sit.

Lame Bear was grateful for this chance to rest. He walked out into the knee-deep grass. There he stretched out full length in the bright sun. He fell into a deep sleep that lasted long into the afternoon. A hot breath on his cheek woke him. He opened his eyes and looked up into the soft brown eyes of Fine Bull's mare.

For the first time, Lame Bear looked at her with real appreciation. She was made better than the average Indian pony. She was taller, with clean, straight legs. Lame Bear liked her deep girth and broad chest. He doubted there was a horse in the Flathead nation that could catch her in a life or death race. He was sure this was one reason why Fine Bull had insisted he take her on his journey south.

Lame Bear liked her color, too. She was a buckskin, the same soft golden brown of a tanned deer hide, with no white markings. The mare would blend in with her surroundings, making it easier to hide from searching eyes. Buckskins were also noted for their exceptional endurance qualities. Lame Bear was pleased. He passed his hand lovingly down the satin arch of the mare's neck. She responded by nibbling the fringe on his leggings.

"You are a beauty," he said. "My heart swells with pride at the sight of you. With Fleet Foot as my helper and you beneath me, I cannot fail. I wonder what Fine Bull calls you?"

"Her name is Fawn." It was Fine Bull. He had been watching Lame Bear and the mare. "As a foal she was very small. The way she pranced and danced reminded

me of a fawn. She is swift and wary like the deer. If you watch her, you will never be caught by an enemy."

Lame Bear gave the mare a final pat on the neck. "Eat well and rest," he said. "Tomorrow we will start the long journey south."

Fine Bull and Lame Bear set up a camp for the night. They spent the evening smoking good tobacco, eating wild meat, and talking about Fine Bull's many adventures. Lame Bear gazed dreamily into the fire, his mind traveling miles away to the south. Tomorrow he would start his own adventure. The thought made his spine tingle. That night he stayed awake for a long time staring up at the star-filled sky, emotions swelling in his chest.

At the first hint of light, Lame Bear was up and packing his gear. He ate breakfast in haste, and very little conversation passed between him and the old man. After the food was eaten, Lame Bear caught the horses, and gave the mare a close inspection. He was satisfied. She was in top condition and eager to go.

Lame Bear turned and faced Fine Bull. A look of mutual understanding passed between them, and then Lame Bear was on the mare's back. Turning her to the south, he gave her a gentle squeeze with his legs. She moved into a ground-eating trot that would take them miles away before sunset. Fine Bull watched the departing figures until they were out of sight, then he turned his own horse back toward the village.

The brilliant blue sky and cool breeze lifted Lame Bear's spirits. Very little escaped his searching eyes as he covered the miles southward. The sun was not far above the horizon when he reached the Belly River. Lame Bear and Fawn crossed without incident and went on their way. Deer and elk grazed in the open meadows. It thrilled him to watch them as he rode along.

The sun rose higher in the sky. Lame Bear began paying more attention to the landscape on his right. He was soon rewarded by the sight of Chief Mountain rising boldly up out of the surrounding hills. As Lame Bear rode on, he felt as if the mountain was watching him, sizing him up to see if he could accomplish the task before him. Sitting a little straighter, he hurried Fawn on her way, anxious to get the mountain behind him.

The trail led into the foothills. Gradually Lame Bear became aware of a distant, dull rumble. As Fawn leaned into the climb, the rumble grew into a loud roar. Suddenly, the trail broke through the trees onto a bluff overlooking a deep gorge. The clear, running waters of Swift Current Creek raged past Lame Bear. He marveled at the frothing, foaming energy of it. He followed the creek the rest of the day, making several detours around the fallen timber that blocked the trail.

The western sky was turning a pinkish gray when Lame Bear broke timberline. He was met by a cold blast of air coming down from the snowfields that stay year-round in the high country. Stopping Fawn, he reached down to unroll his buffalo robe and throw it around his shoulders. And the mare needed a chance to catch her breath.

Lame Bear spoke as he patted her neck. "Today is just the beginning, girl. We will camp here tonight. We both need to be rested before we enter the land of the Flatheads."

Urging Fawn forward, he scouted the slope leading to Swift Current Creek Pass. Finally, he found a good place to camp where the sheer rock wall of the mountain leaned out, creating an overhang with a cozy little hollow underneath. He unpacked his belongings and turned the mare loose to graze on the coarse, high-mountain grass. After a vigorous roll, she got up, shook herself, then settled down to eat. Lame Bear was glad to see she had so much energy after their long, hard ride. As for himself, he felt completely drained of strength. It was time for him to get serious about eating, too. First, he would have to catch his dinner. He picked a spot where he could watch the entire slope, and sat down.

Lame Bear did not have to wait long. With the coming of evening, small animals began to move around in search of food. A rabbit appeared from behind a bush at the base of the cliff. Unsure of the horse, it poked its head out, then drew it back quickly. Its ears and nose were in constant motion as it tested the air for any hint of danger. The rabbit did not see the still form of Lame Bear, nor did the air carry any message of danger, so it hopped out into the open. The light was fading fast. Lame Bear made his move. "Sorry, little brother, but I need the strength that you can give me."

His knife throw was swift and sure. The rabbit never knew what hit it. Lame Bear returned to the overhang and built a small fire to roast the rabbit. One by one the stars began to appear, shining with a special brilliance in the thin mountain air. After finishing his meal, Lame Bear caught Fawn and tied her to a small tree near the overhang. Then gathered enough bear grass to make a soft bed. He crawled under his buffalo robe and fell instantly asleep.

Lame Bear woke to the sound of Fawn pawing the ground. She was cold, hungry, and wanted to be turned loose. He threw back his robe, sucking in his breath as the cold mountain air hit his warm body. "No wonder you are angry with me, Fawn. It seems that winter is hiding in these high places."

Fawn tossed her head and nickered. When Lame Bear

turned her loose, she spent several minutes running and bucking just to get warmed up. As for himself, he hurried back to his bed and threw the buffalo robe around his shoulders. There was not time for a fire. He wanted to get an early start.

Sitting cross-legged under his robe, Lame Bear ate what was left of the cooked rabbit. The eastern sky turned from gray, to pink, to gold, signaling it was time for him to go. He gathered his belongings and caught his reluctant mare. As far as she was concerned, breakfast was not yet over. A sharper than usual nudge in the ribs from Lame Bear got her attention, and she settled down to the business at hand. They headed for the notch in the rugged wall of mountains. This marked the entrance to Swift Current Creek Pass.

A half-mile of rough trail brought them to the summit. Crossing over, they started the long descent down the other side. Lame Bear's heart began to beat faster at every step. He was now treading on enemy ground. The thought made him uncomfortable. He was not used to the idea of someone trying to kill him, nor could he picture himself killing anyone else. He smiled briefly as he thought of the Flatheads trembling at the sound of his name. Well, maybe someday, but right now they would be shaking with laughter if they knew he was coming.

He heard the sound of a creek running off to his right. The trail followed along the water's edge most of the way down into the valley. This would make Lame Bear's travel easier, but the gurgling of the rushing water might also muffle the sounds of an approaching enemy. Lame Bear paid special attention to Fawn, watching her ears as they flicked back and forth. Any change in her behavior would warn him of danger ahead.

The shadows lengthened. Lame Bear looked for a

place to camp. He did not want to camp too close to the valley. The trees were beginning to thin out, and he rode out on the shore of a large mountain lake. Fawn dropped her head to graze while he sat and admired the scenic beauty.

The loud scolding of a squirrel reminded him he was a trespasser here. He pulled Fawn's head up and urged her to go on. The trail skirted the edge of the long lake. It was dusk before they reached its end. He did not want to camp near the trail, so he crossed the outlet and rode around to the opposite shore, and far back into the trees. There he dismounted and tied Fawn. Tonight he would pull grass for her. He could no longer risk letting her run free to graze. Lame Bear did not want to lose her, nor did he want her to be seen. In the morning, he would scout for signs of Flathead hunting parties, and most important, for signs of the wild horse herds.

Chapter Seven

The Medicine Hat Stallion

There was no hint of light in the eastern sky when Lame Bear got up. He set himself immediately to the task of pulling a large mound of grass for Fawn. His fast pace warmed him quickly, and it was not long before Fawn was eating contentedly from the pile of grass he placed before her. Then he took some dried meat from his pack and sat down to his own cold breakfast. He would leave as soon as the mare finished her feed.

Dawn cast a golden glow across the tops of the mountains. Lame Bear mounted Fawn and rode back the way he had come the night before. He crossed the outlet and headed down the trail. Not long after leaving the lake, Lame Bear rode out into the Flathead valley. The creek he was following led him to the Flathead River. He pulled Fawn up and studied the terrain. He decided to cross the river so he could stay close to the range of mountains on the other side. He did not want to be caught out in the open.

After crossing the river, Lame Bear followed it until its southern route started pulling away from the mountains. He and Fawn moved away from the river and headed north. He had not forgotten what Fine Bull told him. The horse he was looking for was somewhere to the north.

Lame Bear spent the rest of the day exploring. He

skirted the southern tip of the mountains, riding into and out of canyons and draws. His main concern was to familiarize himself with the new country he was in. He took special note of good places to hide and to camp. He found old horse droppings on several of the game trails he explored, and a few old campsites, but nothing that indicated the presence of hunting parties this spring. He hoped the Flathead hunting parties would not be coming this far north until the end of summer. This would give him greater freedom of movement.

On the third day of travel, Lame Bear came to a smaller river that joined the Flathead River. He followed it north, hoping to find a favorite watering place for game and wild horses. He was not disappointed. The river he was following ran out of a large lake that all but filled the entrance to a canyon. Lame Bear rode along the western shore of the lake, studying the ground carefully for fresh signs of horses. A break in the canyon wall caught him by surprise. A passageway wide enough to run a herd of buffalo through led to the west, away from the lake. Lame Bear stopped, not sure where to go next.

He decided to follow the lake's tributary to its headwaters. He would come back in a few days to scout the passageway and whatever lay beyond. Lame Bear headed Fawn up the canyon trail, all the while hoping to see some signs of wild horses. After a strenuous day of riding, he made camp. His body ached all over and his heart was sick with disappointment. He had not seen any signs of horses since he entered the Flathead valley. Maybe the whole thing was a big story, and he would have to return to his people in disgrace. He could not bear the thought.

Lame Bear stared into the flames of his small fire. His thoughts returned to his father's lodge. How he longed

to see his father's strong face and his mother's warm smile. He could almost smell the wonderful aroma of the woodsmoke and cooking meat that filled their tipi. He wondered if they missed him, and how Fine Bull was explaining his absence. Loneliness settled over Lame Bear like a dark cloud. A tear rolled down his cheek and dropped unnoticed on the back of his hand. The flames of the fire flickered and sputtered, then died. The glowing embers were reflected in the dark pools of Lame Bear's eyes, and for a moment, his tortured soul twisted his handsome face in agony.

The emotions of the night were etched on Lame Bear's face. He woke up cold and miserable. The sky was gray, promising rain. Fawn nickered softly and nuzzled his shoulder when he brought her an armful of grass. He stroked her soft, warm neck and leaned his head against her shoulder. "Maybe we should forget this crazy idea and go home. No! I could never go home like this. It would be better to ride south and never return than to face my father in shame."

Words of bitterness and frustration poured out of him. The mare stood silently and listened. After a while, he felt empty. He lost all sense of time and purpose. The mare grew restless and pulled away from him. Lame Bear stood staring at her, his mind off in another world.

Suddenly, the silence was broken by the harsh call of a large, grey, bird. At first, Lame Bear did not notice the calling, but something deep in his memory prodded him back to the present. He remembered his little friend from Thunder Mountain. A smile wiped the gloom from his face.

"So, little brother, you have come to cheer me up. It is good to see you again. Maybe you can tell me where the wild ones are hiding," Lame Bear said.

The bird sat listening to Lame Bear, cocking its head from side to side as the youth spoke. Its little black eyes held a mischievous gleam. The bird squawked and flew down the trail. Lame Bear quickly mounted Fawn. He urged her to move as swiftly as possible after the bird. All of his gloomy thoughts were left behind. He was filled with a sense of excited expectation.

They reached the northern shore of the lake by midday. Lame Bear stopped Fawn and searched the forest for the bird. He soon spotted it up in a tree near the western passage. The bird sat preening its feathers, completely ignoring him.

Lame Bear spoke to it. "Are you playing games with me, little brother, or do you have something to show me?" The bird stared at him, never blinking an eye.

"All right, be that way. I will find them myself," he said.

Lame Bear dismounted in disgust. A rock he stepped on gave way and he fell to the ground. The bird squawked and chattered. Lame Bear grinned sheepishly. Then he saw it! There, on the ground next to his hand, was a fresh horse track. For a moment he thought maybe it was Fawn's, but a closer look showed him it was too big to be hers. His heart pounded as he got up and searched the area for more tracks. He was soon rewarded by the signs of a milling horse herd. There were tracks going everywhere.

One track in particular caught his attention. The imprint made by the frog of the hoof was crooked. The bottom of the hoof had probably been cut badly when the horse was a foal, leaving it with a permanently deformed foot. Because of this track, the herd would be easy to follow and locate. He must find out now if this herd was led by the Medicine Hat stallion.

A loud clap of thunder opened up the skies. The rain began to pour down as the mountain storm got under way. Lame Bear mounted Fawn and started circling, hoping to find which direction the herd had come from before the rain washed the tracks away. He was not too surprised when he found them heading into the western passage. Eagerly, he urged Fawn into the gap in the mountains. He was so intent on following the horse tracks, his did not notice his rain-soaked buckskins sticking to his body, or his chattering teeth.

The tracks of the wild herd led Lame Bear to the banks of the Still Water River. There they turned north and followed close to the mountains. Lame Bear knew the herd would be seeking shelter in one of the many draws running into the hills. Rather than wear himself and Fawn out searching for them, he decided to seek shelter, too, and wait out the storm. The horses would come out to graze in the valley as soon as the storm blew over.

He turned Fawn into the first draw he came to, rode into the woods, and stopped under a short, thick-boughed tree. In spite of the dampness, Lame Bear felt warm and happy. In a few hours, he would know whether or not his search was in vain.

The storm ended as quickly as it had begun. The late afternoon sun broke through the clouds. A brilliant rainbow arched across the valley. Lame Bear inhaled the pungent smell of wet pine needles and earth. It filled him with vigorous energy. He swung his arms and flexed his legs to warm up his body, and loosen the wet, sticky, buckskins he wore. He left Fawn tied to a tree, and walked out of the draw to find a place where he could see as much of the valley as possible.

He soon found a small knoll near the river. He climbed up the side and lay down so he could peek over without being seen. Lame Bear tried to keep his mind and eyes on the valley, but the sun's warmth soon made him sleepy. His mind wandered in wonderful dreams of victory until he dozed off into a blissful slumber.

Slowly a new sound began to penetrate his drowsy mind. It was a familiar and soothing sound. For a moment, Lame Bear thought he was back in the Blackfeet camp tending his father's horses. It was the sound a grazing horse makes as its lips gather and its teeth tear a mouthful of grass.

Every nerve in Lame Bear's body came alive. He held his breath and listened. There was a grazing horse near him. Then he heard the unmistakable high-pitched whinny of a foal, and the deep-throated answering nicker of its mother. Lame Bear slowly inched his way forward to look over the top of the knoll. He had to blink several times to get the sleep out of his eyes and adjust them to the late afternoon sun, and the scene before him. Grazing on the lush, green grass was a small band of mares and foals. He was surprised at how few mares there were; yet they were all horses any warrior would be proud to own. The stallion that led this band had chosen his mares well.

Two foals broke away from the herd, bucking and playing. Lame Bear caught his breath. One of them was carrying the markings of a Medicine Hat! This band of mares must belong to the Medicine Hat stallion, but where was he?

Lame Bear knew the stallion would not be grazing with the mares, but would be off by himself where he could watch for signs of danger. He looked everywhere, but there was no sign of him. This worried Lame Bear. He knew a range stallion could be as dangerous as a grizzly bear if he felt himself or his band threatened. He had heard stories of stallions having to be killed before any horses could be taken from their herds. Lame Bear did not like being in the position of not knowing where the horse was.

A loud, warning snort froze him to the spot. He dared not move. The stallion was only a few feet behind him. He could hear the horse drawing in air through flared nostrils, studying the strange creature in front of him. The stallion pawed the ground in frustration.

Lame Bear knew he had to do something to ease the horse's tension. This first meeting between himself and the Medicine Hat was very important. What he did in the next few moments would determine whether or not he would ever be able to gain the stallion's trust. He began to talk to the horse.

"Easy, proud warrior. I did not come here to hurt you. I want to be your friend. You are a great horse and your mares are very beautiful," he said.

At the first sound of the human voice, the stallion's ears flattened and the whites of his eyes showed danger-ously. He snorted and stepped forward. Lame Bear swal-lowed hard and kept talking, trying to keep his voice steady and calm.

"You are a brave horse," he said. "It would be an honor for me to ride you on the warpath. Together, we could bring victory to my father's lodge. You will like my father. He is a wise and brave man."

Slowly, the stallion began to relax. He flicked his ears back and forth, puzzled by this new sound. It troubled him, yet there was something soothing about it, too. It was almost dark before the Medicine Hat dropped his head to take a mouthful of grass. Gradually, he grazed away from Lame Bear and returned to his mares.

Lame Bear let his breath out slowly. He was totally

drained of energy. His muscles ached from being in one position for so long. He rolled over on his back, letting the tension ease from his body. The stars appeared, and remembering Fawn, Lame Bear forced himself to get up. She would be hungry, and nervous from being tied up alone for so long. He must get her fed and watered. Then, he must think of a way to capture the Medicine Hat stallion.

Chapter Eight

War Chief Decides

Lame Bear spent the next few days following the wild herd, learning their habits and patterns of movement. He stayed well out of sight so he would not disturb their daily routine. But he had a feeling the Medicine Hat knew he was there. Often the horse would leave his mares and disappear. Lame Bear was never sure where he went, but he knew the horse was watching him. This pleased him. He wanted the wild horse to get used to him and his presence near the herd.

He still did not know how he was going to capture and gentle the wild stallion. He could not use brute force. It would take much more than one boy to capture the Medicine Hat against his will. No, there had to be another way. But for the time being, his only plan was to get the herd to accept him.

The first few times he approached the horses, they panicked and ran, led by a black mare. Lame Bear noticed that the black mare limped. She must be the horse with the injured hoof. He admired her intelligence. When leading the herd in their mad dash to escape him, she would always take them out into the open, away from places where there might be traps. It was easy to see this mare had been chased by humans before. She knew all of their tricks.

Gradually, the herd became less and less alarmed when Lame Bear and Fawn appeared on the horizon. They did not put much effort into running. One day they did not run at all. The black mare gave a warning snort, which brought all the horses to attention, but they held their ground. Lame Bear kept his eye on the black mare. When she showed signs of fear, he stopped Fawn and waited for the wild mare to relax. Then he let Fawn drop her head to graze. One by one, the wild mares went back to their eating. The black mare was the last one to start grazing again. She grabbed a quick mouthful and then jerked her head up to watch Lame Bear with wary eyes.

Lame Bear felt tense and nervous himself. He knew the Medicine Hat might charge him at any time. He doubted Fawn could escape the stallion's charge, and if the mare fell, he would be trampled to death. Whenever the stallion came too close to him, Lame Bear would begin to talk. The sound of his voice always calmed the wild horse.

"Hello, brave warrior. We meet again. We will be friends someday. You will see," Lame Bear would say. On and on the conversation went, until the stallion returned to his mares.

After several weeks the stallion and Lame Bear relaxed. He decided it was now safe to approach the herd on foot. The next day, he left Fawn tied to a tree and walked to the herd alone. Their reaction was one of complete panic. The black mare threw up her head, gave a warning whistle and bolted. The entire herd went with her. Lame Bear sighed with disappointment. He had hoped his appearance on foot would not frighten them. Now he had to go through the process of conditioning them to his presence all over again.

After a week of walking to the horses, they stopped

running from him. He would sit in the grass for hours, watching them and talking to them. He learned their different personality traits, and he could recognize their voices when they called to each other.

The foals were the first to completely overcome their fear of Lame Bear. He would sit as still as a stone while one or two of them approached him. It was fun to watch them work up their courage to come close enough to smell him. They would come with halting steps, necks outstretched, nostrils flared, until one of them would shy away, causing the whole bunch to wheel and run. This continued for quite some time, until the little black-and-white Medicine Hat actually touched Lame Bear's sleeve with his muzzle.

He was the bravest of the group. Lame Bear held his breath, not wanting to break the magic of the moment. He could feel the foal's warm breath on his face, and see the quizzical expression in the soft, brown eyes. Without warning the colt grabbed a mouthful of leather and tugged. Lame Bear lost his balance and went sprawling, scattering baby horses in all directions. He lay in the grass, laughing, and happier than he had been in a long time.

The carefree days slipped by until it was midsummer. Lame Bear still had not made any progress with the Medicine Hat stallion. The horse tolerated Lame Bear's presence with the herd, but he would not allow the boy to come near him. The passing of time began to worry Lame Bear. If he did not do something soon, he would lose all hope of taking the stallion. The very thought of failure tied his stomach in knots. He must do something, but what?

Lame Bear did not realize it would be Fawn who would give him the help he needed in winning the stallion. It was early morning. Lame Bear went to turn

Fawn loose to graze. Instead of her usual welcoming nicker, she laid her ears back at him and swung her hindquarters in his direction. Lame Bear stopped short, hurt by this strange rebuff from the mare. "Fawn, what is wrong? Are you sick or are you lonesome?"

His gentle voice was met by a sour look from the mare. She pulled roughly away from Lame Bear as he turned her loose. He was puzzled by this strange behavior. He remembered Fawn being moody a couple of times before, but never this bad. As Lame Bead thought back, his face lit up. Of course! The mare was coming into season. The nearness of the stallion, combined with her forced confinement, had set her nerves on edge. This accounted for her cranky behavior.

An idea began to form in Lame Bear's mind as he recalled Fine Bull's wise words. He would use Fawn to win the great stallion's heart. If the horse would not let him approach, then Lame Bear would make the stallion come to him. The idea filled him with joy. He laughed out loud.

Lame Bear decided to put his plan into immediate action. He caught Fawn, who snorted her displeasure at having her breakfast interrupted, and led her out to the wild herd. Locating the stallion, Lame Bear went as close as he dared without causing the horse to leave. He stopped and hobbled Fawn's front legs. Then he took off his shirt, tied it around the mare's neck and walked away.

Fawn watched him leave, but only for a moment. She turned to face the stallion, nickering softly to him. Lame Bear had left her upwind from the Medicine Hat. The breeze soon brought her scent to the stallion. The soft nicker, combined with the strong scent of the mare, got the horse's instant attention. His nostrils flared wide.

With arched neck and prancing step, he approached the hobbled mare.

The stallion danced around Fawn, squealing and nickering. He was plainly puzzled by her immobility. He circled closer and closer until their noses touched. Then, catching Lame Bear's scent, the stallion wheeled and ran. But his desire for the mare kept bringing him back. He pawed the ground in frustration. Finally, he made a savage lunge at the mare, trying to drive her away from the horrible man-scent. Fawn leaped awkwardly, almost falling as the stallion hit her in his charge.

Lame Bear held his breath. He had not thought the stallion might hurt her because of his scent. He drew an arrow and strung his bow. He knew he would kill the Medicine Hat rather than let him harm Fawn.

The Medicine Hat whirled to come at Fawn again. The mare stood wide-eyed, trembling in fear. Lame Bear's heart was in his throat. The stallion charged. Fawn crouched, ready to leap aside at the last moment. Lame Bear pulled back his bowstring, his eyes focusing on a spot just behind the stallion's shoulder. But the arrow was never released. In mid-stride, the Medicine Hat came to a sliding stop, then veered away from Fawn. Lame Bear slowly released the tension on the bowstring, and sighed his relief. Surely the mare sighed, too.

The Medicine Hat spent the rest of the day courting Fawn. He was constantly tormented and perplexed by the presence of Lame Bear's shirt around the mare's neck. In desperation, he grabbed it in his teeth and tried to tear it away. He nearly pulled the mare off her feet, but the shirt stayed. By the end of the day the shirt no longer bothered the stallion. That night Lame Bear returned with Fawn to his camp. He felt as if a great burden had been lifted from his shoulders.

The next morning, Lame Bear went to the mare and untied her. He spoke to her as he patted her neck. "Well, Fawn, you did it. If we succeed in nothing else, at least you will have a foal to present to Fine Bull next spring. You have served me well."

With one final pat on the mare's neck, he slipped his catch rope off over her head and released her. Fawn looked at him, not sure of his intentions.

"Go on, join the herd. You have earned a rest," he said.

The mare hesitated only for a moment before she wheeled away from Lame Bear and ran to join the wild herd.

As the days grew hotter, the herd moved into the canyons and draws to escape the heat and the flies. Their days were spent in the shade of the trees where, head to tail, they fought the persistent deerflies and horseflies. In the cool of the evening they would move out into the open meadows to graze.

Lame Bear was always near the horses. Game was plentiful. He never had to go far to find food. The gooseberries and raspberries were starting to ripen, and gave him a pleasant change of diet.

All of his spare time was spent with the Medicine Hat. He would watch the horse for hours, learning his habits and reactions. The more Lame Bear was with the horse, the more his admiration for him grew. He had all of the requirements of a great war horse; courage, speed, endurance, and heart, that special something that enables a horse to go on even after it is physically exhausted. Lame Bear longed to sit astride the strong back and race the wind.

One day, as he sat on a hillside near the stallion, Lame Bear thought of a name for the wild horse. He spoke to the horse as he always did when he was with him.

"You need a proper name, something that will show you are special. I will call you War Chief because you are chief of all the wild horses, and because your color markings make you a sacred war horse," he said.

Lame Bear sat back, pleased with the name he had chosen. "War Chief, do you like your name?" he asked.

The dozing horse raised his head slightly, and shook it up and down. The stallion was only trying to rid himself of flies, but Lame Bear laughed delightedly. "Then War Chief it shall be," he grinned.

Every day, Lame Bear worked his way closer to the wild stallion. As soon as the horse showed any agitation at his nearness, he would stop and sit down. He talked constantly to the stallion, until War Chief was lulled into a state of complete relaxation. His scent no longer seemed to bother the horse.

Finally, Lame Bear decided to push War Chief to the limits of his tolerance. He needed to know exactly how much he and the stallion could trust each other. He approached the horse in his usual fashion, but this time, when the stallion became nervous, he did not stop. Instead, he held out his hand and walked toward the horse's shoulder. War Chief was momentarily confused by this sudden change in routine. Lame Bear took advantage of the stallion's hesitation. With one quick, fluid movement, he was at the horse's side. War Chief gathered himself, ready to spring away, but some invisible force seemed to be holding him where he stood.

Lame Bear put his hand on the stallion's shoulder, talking softly to him all of the time. War Chief flinched at the unfamiliar sensation. It was more than he could tolerate, and he sidestepped quickly away. Lame Bear smiled. "That's all right, my friend. Soon you will learn to enjoy my touch," he said.

He approached War Chief several times during the day. Each time the stallion allowed himself to be touched a little longer. Lame Bear soon found the horse's itchy spots. He scratched them vigorously. War Chief enjoyed this attention. He closed his eyes and stretched out his neck, his lips itching the back of an imaginary horse. In a moment of ecstacy, the stallion reached around and began nuzzling Lame Bear's shoulder.

Lame Bear chuckled. "There, you see? I'm not so bad. I told you that you would learn to enjoy my touch. Now we can be friends."

He began stroking the stallion all over, until the horse accepted his touch on any part of his body. He then walked to War Chief's head and blew his breath into the horse's nostrils. He did this as a form of introduction, the way horses always sniff noses when they meet. Lame Bear knew this was a means of identification. He wanted War Chief to remember what he smelled like, and to associate his scent with kindness and friendship.

Evening came. They were still together. He watched the sun set, his hand resting lightly on the stallion's neck. As the sun sank over the earth's rim, a distant neigh, carried on the evening breeze, reached them. It sent a shiver through Lame Bear, and made War Chief snort defensively. The sound came again, this time louder. It was the warning call of the grey stallion, Fleet Foot!

Chapter Nine

The Black Mare

Lame Bear woke up the next morning feeling tired and edgy. He could not get the haunting neigh of Fleet Foot out of his mind. What did it mean? Perhaps his mind was playing tricks on him, and it was only the wind he had heard. No, it had been Fleet Foot, and it had been a warning. It was almost as if his spirit helper was trying to wake him out of his dream world, and bring him back to reality.

He sat down on a log to think about his situation. The summer was coming to an end. The days were shorter and the evenings were cooler. It would not be long before the summer rainstorms would turn to snow in the high mountain passes. He had to get out of the Flathead valley before this happened.

Also, even though he had come a long way in his relationship with War Chief, he knew the stallion was not ready to submit to him. There was no way he could make the horse leave the valley against his will.

Lame Bear sighed and got up. He was really no better off than before. Now that his time in the valley was coming rapidly to an end, it was time to catch Fawn and keep her with him. He knew he would feel much better having her close at hand. A small seed of fear had been planted the night before. It was prodding him into action. Lame Bear picked up his rope and headed out to the wild herd.

Fawn raised her head and nickered a greeting at Lame Bear's approach. She was glad to see him. His gentle touch and soft voice were always welcome. She did not try to pull away when he slipped his catch rope around her neck, and she followed him quietly away from the herd. Lame Bear smiled and patted her softly on the neck.

"So, you are not the she-bear you used to be. I have seen you standing in the sunshine, dreaming. Is it motherhood that is on your mind?" he asked.

The mare put her nose in the middle of Lame Bear's back and gave him a shove. He laughed, and grabbing a hank of mane, swung up on her back. It was good to be together again.

Lame Bear was glad he caught Fawn when he did. The Medicine Hat was growing restless. Each day he would push the mares farther north, not letting them graze all day as he used to do. Lame Bear would not have been able to keep up with them on foot.

He tried to spend some time with the stallion, but the horse never stayed for very long. He was always on the move, circling the herd and testing the wind. Lame Bear was not too concerned by War Chief's change in behavior. He thought the coming fall might be making the stallion restless. However, his thoughts changed when the black mare began to behave differently, too. Some unseen danger was making her extremely nervous. She would snatch a mouthful of grass, then lift her head to test the wind. Both the black mare and the stallion kept a watchful eye to the south.

Lame Bear was perplexed by their nervousness. He did some scouting around, but could find nothing that

might be making them restless. It worried him that he could not locate the source of their uneasiness.

Then, on one of his early-morning scouting trips, the mystery was solved. Lame Bear had his eyes on the ground, looking for tracks or any other sign which would tell him of the presence of danger. Suddenly, Fawn stopped, almost unseating him. Lame Bear tensed, all of his senses alert. He breathed in deeply and smelled smoke! There, barely visible, a thin wisp of smoke rose above an aspen grove by the river. He quickly reined the mare around and rode back into the cover of the trees.

He was worried, and sure that the smoke coming out of the aspen grove was from a Flathead campfire. He had to find out how many people there were, and what they were doing here. He tied Fawn well back in the trees, and approached the aspen grove as close as he could without losing cover. He watched and waited. The Flatheads must not see him, nor suspect his presence in the valley, but he must know everything about them.

Lame Bear's patience was soon rewarded. Not long after the smoke ceased rising through the trees, six men rode out of the grove. They were mounted on the Flathead's best horses. Lame Bear noted immediately that this was not a war party. Neither the horses nor the men were painted for war. At least they were not looking for trouble, and he felt a little better about their presence in the valley.

If this was not a war party, then they must be a hunting party out looking for fresh meat. All that Lame Bear had to do was keep out of sight until they left the valley. He would have no problems. Yet, something about their appearance bothered him. All of the members of the hunting party were carrying rawhide ropes. What was it they were hunting? Then the awful truth struck Lame

§

Bear. This was no ordinary hunting party. Those men were going after the wild horses!

A terrible blackness swept over Lame Bear. He felt the earth falling away beneath him. "Fleet Foot, Fleet Foot, where are you? Help me, please!"

It was very quiet. The whole world seemed to be holding its breath, waiting for what was going to happen. War Chief and the black mare had known all along that the Flatheads were coming. They had known for weeks.

The men riding north along the river were soon out of sight. Lame Bear ran as fast as he could back to Fawn. He stumbled and fell several times in his frantic dash for the mare. With pounding heart and spinning head, he climbed on Fawn's back and headed north, too. He galloped headlong through the trees, dodging and weaving to miss the branches. He must reach the horses before the Flatheads found them. Somehow, he must hide them from the hunters.

Lame Bear underestimated the speed at which the hunting party was able to travel. By the time he reached the herd's location, the Flatheads had surrounded the wild horses in a halfcircle that would force the herd to run south, back down the valley. Lame Bear wanted desperately to warn the horses of the approaching danger, but his position made it impossible. It would be foolish to reveal himself now that the trap was already being sprung on the herd. He looked on in helpless frustration, not hearing the sob that wrenched from his throat.

War Chief was the first to sense the herd's danger. His warning snort brought every horse to attention. The stallion plunged into the herd, scattering mares and foals before him. He headed for the black mare. She saw him coming and bolted to escape his teeth. Several mares followed her. The Medicine Hat's charge came too late.

Before the herd could gather momentum the Flathead riders came charging down on them. Their bloodcurdling yells terrified the horses. The leading mares skidded to a stop, then wheeled around to charge back into their followers. Total chaos resulted, and in a few moments the herd was circling in confusion. War Chief dashed frantically in and out of the herd, biting and kicking, trying to force the mares north.

Only the black mare held to her original course of flight, making a desperate dash for freedom. Two of the horsemen realized her intentions and swung their mounts into the path of her escape, cutting her off. She swung away, but the riders pressed her hard, forcing her to run back into the herd. The black mare never broke stride as she shot through the milling horses and broke out the other side, heading south. The other horses followed her example. Soon the whole herd was running down the valley.

Lame Bear swung Fawn around and kicked her into a run. He knew he would not be able to keep up with the wild horses, but he wanted to stay as close to them as possible. He was hoping the herd could outlast the Flathead ponies in what he knew would be a strenuous run. Their only chance was that they were fresh and riderless. For now, he must concentrate on guiding Fawn through the trees at breathtaking speed.

The Flathead riders pushed the herd hard, using their own horses as if they had endless stamina. Surely they could not hold the pace much longer. But these men were experienced horse hunters. They had come prepared. Just as the herd reached the aspen grove, the riders dashed into the trees, dismounted their exhausted horses, pulled their headgear, and mounted six fresh horses they had left behind that morning.

This took only a few moments. The wild herd never knew they had been left. Soon the riders were back in full pursuit. When the herd showed signs of slowing down the riders moved in on them, forcing them to speed up. The fast pace was beginning to tell on the older mares and the foals. One by one they began to drop out of the race, coming to shaky stops to stand with legs spraddled and sides heaving. The men rode on by them. They were after only the swift and the strong.

The wild herd's dash for freedom was coming to an end. Only a few horses were still running strong. The riders began shaking out their loops, eying the herd to see which one of the horses they wanted for their own. The little Medicine Hat caught the eye of one of the hunters. He was the only foal still running with the herd. He matched his mother stride for stride, little neck outstretched, nostrils flared to a brilliant red, foam flying from his sweat-drenched body, and running his heart out. Admiration for the foal's courage filled the Flathead with desire. He must have the little Medicine Hat!

The black mare saw him coming. Doubling her efforts, she veered sharply to the left, heading for the gap which was now near at hand. Her baby stayed right with her. The hunter followed in swift pursuit, not quite sure what to do next. He wanted to rope the foal, but if he did, chances were the black mare would turn on him to defend her baby. The man had no desire to take on the fury of the wild mare.

To rope the mare was useless. She was a bad one. Over the years, many men had tried to catch her. The ones who had managed to rope her wished they had not. She was wise, independent, and dangerous. One might as well put his rope on a wild, mountain cat as to catch the black mare. Even if she were captured successfully, she would never adapt to captivity. The black mare was more trouble than she was worth.

The Flathead's mind was made up. He must have the Medicine Hat foal. He knew what he had to do to get it. The three horses were now in the passageway, running slower because of the rougher terrain. The rider took advantage of the slower pace. Putting his catch rope under his knee, he removed his bow from across his shoulders and drew an arrow from his quiver.

The black mare broke from the gap and headed straight for the lake. The Flathead moved his horse in on the mare and drew along side of her. For a moment his eyes met hers. She had wild eyes, rimmed in white and filled with hate. The arrow was strung. The bow was drawn. In one terrible moment the deed was done. The arrow made a dull, sickening thud as it entered the mare's rib cage. She took it in silence. With one last great effort, the black mare gathered herself and leaped into the lake. There was a brief struggle, then all was still. The black body floated gently to the surface of the water.

When the Medicine Hat foal reached the shore of the lake, he froze, exhausted and confused. His flight had been directed solely by his mother, and now that she was gone, he was completely lost. With his senses dulled by the blood pounding in his ears and the searing pain in his lungs, the rawhide rope settled unnoticed around his neck. The war bridle was in place before he became aware of the man. The little horse made a feeble attempt to escape, but the man's strength and the painful pressure of the halter were too much for him. In a few minutes, he was leading like a gentle horse, but the Flathead was not fooled. He knew as soon as the foal regained his strength and wind, he would fight like a wildcat. The warrior smiled in anticipation of the battle. This little horse was well worth the sore muscles and bruises he knew he would get before he had him mastered.

By the time the Flathead warrior returned with the Medicine Hat foal, the other hunters had made their catches, too. Only two of the riders remained. They were in hot pursuit of War Chief. The brave stallion darted and dodged away from their ropes, finding extra bursts of speed from deep within his soul. But he was at the disadvantage of running against two fresh horses. War Chief had escaped the Flatheads season after season. By now they knew all of his habits and tricks. They were determined not to lose him this time.

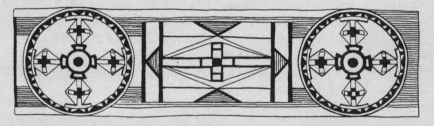

Finally, one of the riders rode in to distract the stallion, and the other one closed in from the other side. An expertly thrown loop settled over War Chief's head. Before the stallion had a chance to charge his captor, a second loop ensnared his front feet. Both men brought their horses to a quick stop and braced themselves for the horse's impact when he hit the end of the ropes. The result was a sudden and terrible fall for War Chief.

The stallion fought as hard as he could with what little strength he had left, but the rope around his neck was being drawn tighter and tighter. War Chief gasped and gulped, trying in vain to draw air into his lungs. His head pounded, and the earth spun as blackness blocked out his senses.

As soon as the stallion went limp, the rider who had forefooted him leaped off of his horse and ran to War Chief's head. He fashioned a war bridle with his rope, and remounted his own horse. The other rider immediately gave the stallion slack so he could get air.

For a long time War Chief did not move. All of his attention was focused on the simple process of breathing. At last, the stallion came to his feet with a violent lunge. His tormentors had him crosstied between the two ropes. When he charged the rider on his right, the terrible choking returned; and when he charged the rider on his left, the pressure from the war bridle brought sharp pain to his mouth and behind his ears.

The stallion soon learned the lesson of the rope. It was useless to resist its terrible pressures. The two Flathead riders had War Chief under control. They looked at each other, and cut loose with a triumphant war whoop. For now, the victory was theirs.

Chapter Ten

In the Enemy's Camp

The trees and the rough terrain caused Lame Bear to lose sight of the wild herd and their Flathead pursuers. He was frantic with worry, but his most important concern was to keep Fawn from hurting herself or from becoming exhausted. He knew their severest test was yet to come. They would both be required to give their best and more. Finally, impatience got the best of him. He decided to take the risk of being seen for the sake of easier traveling. He turned the mare out of the trees and down into the valley.

Lame Bear soon came upon the exhausted stragglers from the herd. They were too tired even to raise their heads as he passed them. The sight filled him with sadness. He felt especially sorry for the foals. Not only were they physically spent, but they had the added emotional stress of being separated from their mothers. They were old enough to be weaned, but had they been left with their mothers Nature would have been more gentle. The mares would have gradually stopped letting them nurse, and they would have gone off on their own. Now, most of them would probably find their mothers within a few days, but the sight of them was still pathetic.

Fawn's steady canter soon brought them close to the aspen grove where they first saw the Flathead warriors. Lame Bear's heart sank when he spotted the six Flathead ponies grazing nearby. The sweat on their backs had not completely dried yet. Any hope he had for the horses was now gone. He urged Fawn on, anxious to find out what had become of the herd.

The shadows were lengthening when Lame Bear came upon more members of the herd. They were grazing and resting near the river. He knew that as soon as they recovered their strength they would head north, picking up stragglers as they went.

Lame Bear kept count of the horses as he rode down the valley. So far, they were all there except for War Chief, the black mare, her foal, a buckskin, a roan, and a bay. He knew it would take more than one man to handle War Chief and the black mare, so one of them must have escaped. He hoped it was War Chief, yet he knew the Flatheads would give up all of the other horses before letting the stallion escape.

Speaking to Fawn, he said, "These Flatheads are not fools. They have taken the best of the herd. Now we will see if they can keep them."

Lame Bear dismounted and began searching the ground for signs of what had happened. He figured the Flatheads had a camp to the south, but he needed to know for sure. In the morning, they would come back for their extra horses. Whatever he was going to do, he had to act now, while the men and their horses were exhausted from the day's work.

He soon found a spot where a terrific struggle had taken place. The earth was torn up in a great circle. Then he saw where a horse had fallen. What horse had fought so hard? In his heart, Lame Bear knew, but his mind was not willing to accept the idea. Tracks showed that the struggling horse was being forced southward.

Lame Bear took Fawn to the river for a quick drink,

then mounted and headed south at a brisk trot. He hoped to find the Flathead camp before nightfall, but darkness closed in around him, forcing him to slow his pace. He had to move carefully for fear of blundering into the Flatheads. He must be able to catch them off-guard if his plan was to succeed.

He rode close to the river, counting on its noise to cover any sounds he made. He figured the horsemen would have their camp somewhere near the fresh-running water. He figured right. Up ahead he saw the flickering light of a campfire. Soon, the smell of camp smoke and roasting meat reached his nostrils. The hot pain in his stomach reminded him that he had not eaten all day. But he forgot his discomfort when he thought of the task before him.

Lame Bear tied Fawn in a grove of willows and proceeded on foot along the bank of the river. First, he must locate the six warriors before he could do anything about the horses. He found them, as he hoped he would, sitting around the fire eating fresh-roasted meat. They were not expecting trouble. No guard was posted. They were telling stories, and laughing at each other's wild adventures. Relaxed and full of good food, the men were soon spread out on their buffalo robes.

Waiting was hard, but Lame Bear made sure the Flatheads had plenty of time to sink into deep sleep before he made his next move. Crawling on his stomach, he moved in closer to the camp. In the darkness it was hard to locate the horses. Then he heard a plaintive little nicker from out beyond the camp. Lame Bear recognized it immediately as the Medicine Hat foal. He waited for an answering nicker to come from the black mare, but it never came. He wondered where she was.

Now that he had located the horses, Lame Bear was

not quite sure what to do with them. They were all wearing hobbles, and the wild ones had ropes running from their hobbles to a strong stake in the ground. He knew they would go crazy with fear if he got close enough to cut them loose. The only wild horse he had any chance of getting close to was War Chief, but first he must turn the Flathead ponies loose.

The Flathead horses were grazing in a bunch by themselves. Lame Bear approached them slowly, talking softly to reassure them. He took out his knife and moved swiftly from horse to horse, cutting the hobbles as he went. Then quietly, he started herding them southward. Even though they were tired and hungry, he knew their instinct to head home was strong. He was not disappointed. Soon they broke into a trot that would take them far away by morning. For now, his enemies were left to travel on foot.

All of this time, sharp eyes watched him. War Chief was poised, ready to attack the two-legged creature if he dare come near enough. The stallion was worked into a rage. He hated the ropes and he hated the men who used them. Most of his strength was returning with the few hours of rest and food since the Flatheads made camp. But he had learned his lesson well. He would not allow the ropes to down him again.

Lame Bear made a hard decision. He would free only War Chief, leaving the others behind. He must also leave the foal. The stress of another hard run would kill him. As for the other three horses, he knew that their fighting and struggling would wake the Flatheads before he could cut them loose. It was not worth the risk. Freeing War Chief would be dangerous enough.

He circled around the stallion, stopping when he was upwind from him. He wanted to make sure his scent reached the horse long before he did. War Chief never took his eyes off of Lame Bear. His nostrils flared, drawing at the breeze, trying to pick up the enemy's scent. He stood, ready to charge as soon as Lame Bear came within reaching distance. His eyes blazed and his muscles quivered in anticipation.

Approaching in the dark, Lame Bear was unaware of the stallion's intentions. His courage would have failed him if he had seen the horse's terrible expression. He had complete faith that War Chief would accept him. It was this blind faith that would save his life. He was counting on their past friendship to overcome War Chief's fear.

Walking slowly with his hand outstretched, Lame Bear came to the stallion. "Take it easy, proud warrior. I want to help you. I want to be your friend. Tonight we can bring honor to the Blackfeet people. Oh, please do not fight me!"

Lame Bear was now in easy reach of War Chief, but the stallion did not move. His instinct was to fight, yet this was the voice of a friend. This human's scent brought back gentle memories of his mares, and of his peaceful valley. Gradually, the stallion's muscles relaxed and his stance straightened. He stretched out his neck and sniffed gently at the offered hand.

Lame Bear sighed with relief. "So, we are still friends. Now we will see how deep your friendship goes."

He stroked War Chief's neck. Lame Bear was glad to see that the Flatheads had left the war bridle on the stallion. As hard as it was to think so, he was still thankful for the lesson they gave War Chief about ropes. It was making his job much easier.

Taking the lead rope in one hand, Lame Bear reached down with his other hand and quickly cut the hobbles loose from the stallion's front legs. Then he pulled on the lead rope, praying War Chief would not fight him. With the first tug on the rope, War Chief threw up his head and rolled his eyes, resisting the pressure of the bridle. He spoke softly, encouraging the horse to follow him. A second tug, and War Chief took a few hesitant steps forward. After several more tugs on the lead rope, the stallion followed at Lame Bear's heels.

His plan was working well, almost too well. Lame Bear was thankful, but he could not believe his good fortune would last forever. His enemies were without horses, and at last his beloved stallion was by his side. What could go wrong now? The answer soon came.

Lame Bear was leading War Chief close to the riverbank, and was in sight of the willows where Fawn was tied. A soft breeze was blowing their way, bringing the mare's scent to the stallion. Lost in his thoughts, Lame Bear was not paying attention to the breeze or the horse. War Chief caught Fawn's scent and neighed loudly. Fawn, glad to hear from a friend, whinnied high and shrill. The four horses back in the Flathead camp, seeing they were being left, neighed their desperate reply. For a moment all was quiet and still. Then the night exploded.

Almost as one man, the six Flathead warriors were on their feet, weapons in hand. Lame Bear heard them calling to each other in an unfamiliar tongue. The confusion in their voices soon turned to anger, as they discovered the cut hobbles and their horses gone. Their angry shouts spurred Lame Bear into action. He ran to where Fawn was tied, and freeing her, tried to mount, but the two excited horses were making it impossible. Fawn kept turning to face the stallion, and with War Chief prancing around, it was all Lame Bear could do to hang on to him. Finally, in fear and frustration, he jerked as hard as he could on their bridles, causing them both sobering pain. Lame Bear took advantage of the moment to get mounted. He pulled Fawn sharply around and kicked her into a trot, not daring a faster gait for fear War Chief would get out of control.

The Flathead warriors gathered around their fire in helpless frustration. There was not a horse in camp they could ride in pursuit. They did not even have an idea who they were going to pursue, or how many there were, or what direction they should take. The whole situation was very humiliating. All they could do was wait until morning before the mystery could be solved.

In the hours before dawn, Lame Bear put many miles between himself and the Flathead camp. He hoped to have a full day's head start on his pursuers. He needed some time to rest Fawn and War Chief, and to plan what he should do next.

He rode along the Stillwater River until he reached the passageway through the mountains and headed the horses into the gap. Because he was familiar with the country, he decided to return to the lake, and then follow along the mountains to where he had crossed the Flathead River when he came to the valley. From there, he would head for Swift Current Creek Pass and the trail home.

The night had been cold. Lame Bear was chilled, exhausted, and hungry. He wanted more than anything just to lie down and sleep for a few hours. The horses were also tired after their night-long trek. They were almost to the lake when a sudden eruption of scavenger birds startled them out of their exhausted stupor. Fawn stopped so suddenly that Lame Bear almost fell off. War Chief became alert and defensive.

Lame Bear spoke to reassure himself and the horses.

"Easy now. Those birds are just feeding on some poor deer the coyotes have killed. We have nothing to fear."

He urged his horses forward. As they broke out on the shore of the lake, the sight before him caused his empty stomach to heave. He slid weakly from Fawn's back and walked over to the body of the black mare that lay in shallow water. Leaning over, he grabbed the shaft of the arrow that pierced the mare's side and snapped it off. He studied the marking of ownership. Lame Bear burned them into his brain, never to be forgotten.

He stroked the once-proud neck as he spoke. "I will never forget you, black mare. Someday, I will meet the man who made this arrow, and I will make him pay for this terrible thing."

Lame Bear closed his eyes tight to squeeze back the tears. He stood up and threw the broken arrow far out into the lake. He returned to his horses, wearily mounted Fawn, and headed south along the lake's shore. He never looked back.

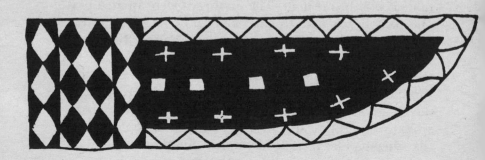

Chapter Eleven

Escape

As soon as there was enough light to see, the six Flathead warriors went to work. One man headed south on the trail of the six Flathead ponies. There was some hope the horses might stop to graze long enough for a swift runner to catch up with them. One man stayed in camp to care for and guard the horses that were left. They could not risk losing them. The remaining four men headed north.

The Flathead warriors followed Lame Bear's tracks to the place where Fawn had been tied in the willows. After studying all of the signs, they determined that they were raided by only one man. The Flatheads were amazed that one person was able to cut loose and control the Medicine Hat stallion. This man was truly a worthy adversary. Another thing that bothered them was the size of the footprints they were tracking. They looked more like those of a boy than a grown man, and one foot came down crooked. They argued among themselves about what this might mean, but they could not accept the idea that they had been raided by a boy. Surely they were on the trail of a rather small but courageous warrior.

The four men broke into a jog. By midmorning, they came upon the six ponies they had turned loose in the aspen grove. In his excitement, Lame Bear had forgotten about them.

The Flathead warriors rejoiced at their good fortune. The men approached the horses very carefully. The horses were reluctant to be caught, but experience had taught them it was futile to resist. Soon the four warriors were mounted and on their way, leading the other two horses with them. Their mood was light. The lone horsethief could not escape them now!

Lame Bear rode in a state of numbness. He had given Fawn her head and was concentrating on staying on her back. He ached all over and his bad leg throbbed painfully. The mare traveled south along the lake's shore. When they reached its outlet, both horses stopped. The lush grass and their exhaustion brought them to a halt, but Lame Bear did not dismount. Fawn reached around and sniffed his foot, then taking the moccasin in her teeth, she began pulling.

The sensation of losing his balance brought Lame Bear to his senses. He dismounted and sank gratefully into the grass. The horses would not wander away. They were too tired and hungry. He had more than a half-day's head start on his enemies. Besides, they were on foot. He would rest only a few hours and then be on his way again. Feeling safe with these thoughts, Lame Bear sank into a deep, deep, sleep.

It was cold, so cold. Where was his buffalo robe? If only his mother would let him sleep a little longer. His leg hurt and it was such a long walk out to the horse herd. Lame Bear tossed and turned, not wanting to give up his sleep, but it was cold and his belly was on fire. He opened his eyes reluctantly, and then he remembered. He was not at home in his father's lodge but in a hostile land, alone, and hungry.

Lame Bear sat up slowly, rubbing his eyes. Sometime during his sleep the sky had clouded up. The clouds were not the big white thunderheads of a summer storm. They were the solid, grey mass of a cold front coming down from the north. The wind had a bite to it. Lame Bear knew from experience this storm was going to leave snow in the high mountain passes. He also knew he had to ride hard before he would reach Swift Current Creek Pass. He would have to beat the storm if he wanted to see his home again.

The two horses were grazing where he had left them. Lame Bear was glad to see they were looking much better after their rest. This would be their last good feed before they reached home. He looked at the sky again, and frowned. He had slept too long. It was late afternoon and would soon be dark. He needed to find food and the horses could use more rest, but the coming storm weighed heavy on his mind. He wanted to keep going, but he dared not risk losing the trail in the dark. Finally, he decided to stay. The Flathead hunters would have to make camp for the night, too. They would not be able to catch up with him on foot, nor could they follow his trail in the dark. Lame Bear felt safe enough to relax his guard and tend to his most immediate need, food!

The Flathead warriors followed Lame Bear's trail at a steady trot. With each mile, they grew more curious about their strange adversary. He was not traveling fast and he was not trying to cover his tracks. Either he was very brave or very foolish. They were even more surprised when the trail entered the passageway to the lake. The men knew this part of the country well. Taking the trail to the lake made no sense for it led nowhere.

They proceeded with caution, fearing an ambush as they approached the lake. They were hoping to catch the horsethief offguard. The sudden flight of a flock of scavenger birds startled them, and shattered their hope of

surprise. One warrior went ahead on foot as a scout, and his sharp whistle soon let the others know it was safe to move ahead.

The Flatheads studied the tracks on the ground carefully. Here was another mystery. Why would anyone show so much interest in the body of the black mare? No man had ever touched her. She had always made trouble for the horse hunters. This man had pulled the arrow from her body. Again the warriors were puzzled. They talked among themselves for some time without coming to any conclusions.

Darkness and a storm were closing in on the mountains. The four men decided to make camp in the shelter of the trees. They had come far and the freshness of the tracks indicated their adversary was not very far ahead of them. They could rest all night and catch up with him easily the next day. The Flathead warriors went to sleep that night, sure of their success.

After a hearty meal of lake trout, Lame Bear tended to his horses. He checked them carefully for sore muscles and injuries. A careful inspection indicated his horses were strong and ready for more hard riding. With the storm coming in, Lame Bear decided to tie the horses up for the night. It would be disastrous to lose them now.

War Chief fought violently when he found himself tied to a tree. However, after several moments of furious struggle, he realized the rawhide rope and the tree were stronger than he was. Lame Bear was glad he was not on the other end of War Chief's lead rope. He could not help wondering what was going to happen the first time he tried to ride the stallion. It was a thrilling, and at the same time, a frightening thought. When the time came he hoped he would have the strength to master War Chief.

Once the horses were settled for the night, Lame Bear

wrapped himself in his buffalo robe, and found shelter from the wind. It was not long before he fell asleep.

At first Lame Bear thought it was the wind. He pulled his robe closer around himself and tried to get back to sleep. There it was again! He lifted his head and strained to hear. The wind was blowing cold and hard. His ears must be playing tricks on him. No, this time he heard it clearly: the urgent, warning neigh of a stallion. But it was not War Chief. Lame Bear held his breath, waiting. It came again, loud and long, sending a chill down his spine. There was no mistaking it now. It was his spirit helper, Fleet Foot, and the message was clear. The Flatheads must be very near!

There was barely a hint of light in the eastern sky. Lame Bear gathered his belongings and hurried to the horses. They greeted him with anxious nickers. He allowed them only a short drink, not wanting their bellies to be heavy with water. Then he mounted Fawn, and leading War Chief, headed down the trail at a brisk trot.

By mid-day, Lame Bear had covered half the distance to Swift Current Creek Pass. He watched his back trail carefully, hoping to get a glimpse of his pursuers. He knew they were close, but he needed to know how close. The clouds were lowering and the wind was picking up. The storm would break soon. He was running out of time.

The Flathead warriors were mounted and on the trail south as soon as there was enough light to see the tracks they were following. When they were sure of the direction Lame Bear was taking, they broke their horses into a steady canter. Soon they reached the place where Lame Bear had made his camp. The excitement of the four riders grew as they realized their man was not very far ahead of them. They talked excitedly, and one man pointed to the south. They urged their ponies on, stopping only when they became unsure of the trail.

As the day wore on, the trail that had been taking the Flatheads south turned northeast. The men began to suspect they were on the trail of a Blackfeet. It would bring them great honor to capture such a brave warrior, and to get their horses back. They hurried on, wanting to catch the Blackfeet before the storm broke.

Lame Bear heard the Flathead warriors' victorious yell before he saw them. He looked over his shoulder, then dug his heels into Fawn's sides. She bounded forward and in a few strides was running hard, War Chief by her side. The mare's incredible speed soon put them out of danger, but Lame Bear knew she could not keep up this pace for long. This was her third day of hard riding, with very little rest. Lame Bear recognized the six horses from the aspen grove. They were in good shape and were well rested, too. He knew it was only a matter of time before the warriors would catch up with him.

The Flatheads were surprised by the buckskin mare's speed. She would be a great prize to capture. They were more determined than ever not to let their adversary escape. The warriors wanted to end the chase before their horses began to tire. They did not want to take any chances on how fast the buckskin mare might really be. They decided to send the two best riders ahead on the two unridden horses. The chosen riders moved their horses up beside the fresh mounts, and in one fluid movement, changed horses. The Flathead horses lengthened their stride, and began closing the gap between themselves and the rider in front of them.

Fawn began to tire. Sweat drenched her neck and little flecks of foam flew from her mouth. At this pace she would soon be running on heart alone. Lame Bear decided he would let himself be captured before he would take the chance of running the mare to death. He looked back and saw only two riders. They were closing fast. In an instant he realized what the Flatheads had done. His heart sank. Fawn could never outlast their fresh horses unless . . . No, it was impossible. He could never do it, but for Fawn's sake he had to try. Lame Bear looked over at War Chief. The stallion was running strong, showing no signs of stress.

Nearing the Flathead River, Lame Bear knew what he must do. He would switch horses during the crossing. The stallion would not be bothered by his weight in the water. He just hoped the horse would accept it when they were on the other side. The river loomed up ahead of them. The excited yells of the Flathead warriors rang in Lame Bear's ears. Fawn did not hesitate when she reached the bank, but plunged willingly into the icy water. The stallion stayed right with her. The cold water took their breaths away, but the horses quickly recovered and began swimming strongly.

Lame Bear reluctantly dropped his bow, arrows, and buffalo robe into the river, keeping only his knife. He did not want anything to get in his way when he tried to get on the stallion. The horses were halfway across when he slipped gently from the mare's back and swam over to the stallion. Speaking quiet words of encouragement, he grabbed a handful of mane and slowly pulled himself onto War Chief's back. The stallion flicked his ears back for a moment, telling Lame Bear he knew he was there.

Lame Bear stroked the stallion's wet neck. "Now, War Chief, we will show these Flathead warriors what you can do."

The horses reached the opposite shore and lunged out

of the water. By now rain was coming down in a steady
drizzle. For a moment, both horses stood with sides
heaving, catching their breaths. Lame Bear sat motion-
less, praying War Chief would not buck him off.

The Flathead warriors were on the other shore. Lame
Bear squeezed his legs against the stallion's sides, giving
him the command to go forward. He felt the horse's
muscles tighten and sensed the coming reaction. Lame
Bear gritted his teeth and grabbed as much mane as he
could hold, but nothing happened. Fawn and War Chief
had their heads up, listening and testing the wind. Lame
Bear heard it, too—the familiar, haunting neigh of Fleet
Foot. Fawn nickered a frantic greeting. War Chief
neighed a challenge to the unseen stallion. Now Lame
Bear understood the message. He must keep the mare in
front of him to guide the Medicine Hat.

Lame Bear spoke to her. "Take us home, Fawn." The
mare trotted away from the river, then broke into a canter. War Chief was quick to follow.

The rain was falling harder now, and thick gray
clouds dropped lower on the mountains. It would be
getting dark soon. In the dwindling light, Lame Bear
thought his eyes were playing tricks on him. He thought
he saw another horse running beside Fawn. It looked
like a horse, yet it was more like a shadow. War Chief
was having a hard time keeping up with Fawn. The
stallion stretched out, running hard, but the mare was
keeping an easy lead. Even though Fawn was exhausted,
she was outrunning War Chief! For an instant, Lame
Bear saw clearly the two horses in front of him. Running
beside Fawn, giving her his strength and his speed, was
Fleet Foot. The thrilling sight lasted only a moment.
Then the two horses disappeared into the mist.

Lame Bear was so enchanted by the scene that he

neither heard nor saw the Flathead arrow that barely missed him. By now, the warriors were close enough to see they were chasing a boy instead of a man. The shame of being outsmarted by a mere youth drove them to desperate measures. It they had to kill Lame Bear to get the horses, they would do it. Only the heavy mist saved Lame Bear from a second arrow. They would not miss a third time, given a clear shot.

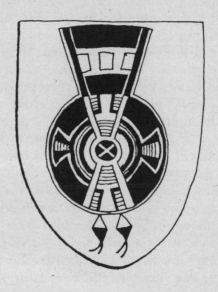

Chapter Twelve

High Places

Red Eagle stood facing the east, watching the sun rise, and praying to the spirits. Then he turned to face the mountains. What a glorious morning! It was that beautiful time of year when the days were no longer hot, nor did they yet have the cold bite of fall. The sky was crystal clear. Fresh snow frosted the tops of the mountains.

Fresh snow. Red Eagle's brow furrowed with worry. It was early summer when Fine Bull had come to him to explain the disappearance of his son. The old man said Lame Bear had gone on a journey across the mountains. He would say no more. It was only Red Eagle's love and respect for the old man that let him trust Fine Bull's judgement concerning Lame Bear's safety. But now he could no longer hide his worry. It was time to move the village south. The snows would be coming soon, and he could not wait for his son much longer.

Fine Bull watched Red Eagle with a heavy heart. He knew what was on the brave warrior's mind, for it was troubling him, too. With or without the Medicine Hat stallion, Lame Bear should have returned by now. The old man had greater worries than the chief. He knew just how dangerous a mission the boy had gone on across the mountains. Fine Bull prayed that for Red Eagle's sake, the spirits would return Lame Bear soon.

The sun was halfway across the sky. Red Eagle climbed up the hillside to get a better view of the trails coming into camp from the west. He sat down and was soon lost in thoughts of his son. How he missed him.

The warrior sat alone for a long time. At first, he did not pay any attention to the sound of a neighing horse. It was probably just one that was separated from the main herd. But the sound persisted, getting louder all the time. Something about it began to bother Red Eagle. It sounded so much like Fleet Foot. No. That was impossible. He searched the treeline anxiously. There was a movement in the trees. He could not tell whether it was a deer, an elk, or a horse. Then he saw that there were two horses, and one was carrying a rider. The chief leaped to his feet and ran down the slope as fast as he could go.

Red Eagle became more excited the closer he got to the two horses. He recognized the buckskin mare as one from Fine Bull's herd. The other horse he had never seen before, but he was sure its rider was Lame Bear. As Red Eagle approached the horses, he slowed down. The rider on the Medicine Hat was in trouble. Red Eagle did not want to make matters worse by causing the horses to run away. He started talking to Fawn as he walked up to her. The mare was standing still, as if in a trance. Red Eagle went to her and began to stroke her neck. He could see plainly now that the slumped-over figure on the Medicine Hat stallion was Lame Bear.

War Chief was completely spent. Only his strong will to survive had kept him going. He refused to let Fawn out of his sight. The stallion's senses were dulled by exhaustion and hunger. It was not until he bumped into Fawn that he realized there was a human standing in front of him. War Chief snorted his alarm, gathering his remaining strength for an attack. He was not going to run anymore.

Red Eagle was saddened by the sight of the two horses. They were gaunt and weak and would need immediate attention if they were to be saved. But he was even more concerned about War Chief's burden. His son was either unconscious or dead. The stallion, with ears back, made it very clear he would not give up the youth without a fight. Red Eagle took Fawn's mane and led her slowly back to camp. War Chief followed behind her.

When he was near camp, Red Eagle yelled to one of the men on guard to get Fine Bull. He wanted everyone else to stay in camp so the stallion would not be made more upset by a crowd of people.

Fine Bull came quickly. He saw in a moment Red Eagle's plight. He spoke softly to the two horses, and then he moved slowly to Fawn's side. The mare nuzzled him, glad to feel his touch and hear his familiar voice. In one graceful move, the old man mounted Fawn and moved her back beside War Chief. The mare's nearness reassured the stallion.

Fine Bull spoke softly, trying to get the horse to relax. "So, we meet again, Medicine Hat. You have grown into a fine horse. Thank you for bringing our son home, but now you must let us have him."

Lame Bear had tied himself onto his horse before he lost consciousness. A piece of rawhide stretched from one wrist under the stallion's neck to the other wrist. Fine Bull took out his knife, leaned over slowly and cut the leather. Then he gently pulled Lame Bear's limp body from War Chief's back, and draped him across the withers of his own horse. Red Eagle took the stallion's lead rope, and together the men returned to the village. They went straight to Fine Bull's tipi.

The chief was first to speak. "Fine Bull, you are wise. Take my son and use your wisdom and powers to save him. I will care for the horses. May we both be successful!"

"I will do all I can for your son." replied Fine Bull. "Lame Bear is a chosen one. The Earth Powers have a plan for his life. I do not think it is his time to die."

Red Eagle went away from Fine Bull's lodge reassured. In the meantime, he must use his own wisdom in caring for the horses. With proper attention, they would recover from their ordeal and be as sound as when they started.

For several days Lame Bear floated in and out of consciousness. He was so cold. Where was his buffalo robe? Snow. Everywhere there was snow. He could not see. Where was Fawn? He must not lose Fawn. "Fawn, wait for me! Don't leave me! Fleet Foot . . . !"

Lame Bear was near death. Fine Bull worked continually on him, sleeping only for brief periods of time. He kept the boy's body surrounded with hot rocks wrapped in furs, as it was incapable of producing its own heat. Hour after hour, the old man forced spoonsful of hot broth between Lame Bear's trembling lips. Gradually the chills became less violent, and Lame Bear sank into a deep, deep sleep.

For a long time, Lame Bear lay with his eyes closed, testing his senses. He was alive! He was warm and he was hungry. He opened his eyes slowly and turned his head toward the fire. Fine Bull was sitting there, smoking his pipe, thinking faraway thoughts.

"How long have I been here?" Lame Bear asked.

The sound of his voice breaking the silence startled Fine Bull. He coughed on his smoke. "Welcome back, my son," he said. "The sun has risen and set ten times since you came to my tipi."

Lame Bear was full of questions. "How did I get here? The horses! Where are the horses?"

Fine Bull patiently answered all of his questions, telling him the horses were healthy and strong.

"War Chief. I must see War Chief." Lame Bear tried to rise, but fell back, too weak to hold himself up.

"Who is War Chief?" asked the old man, with a twinkle in his eyes.

"War Chief is the Medicine Hat," replied Lame Bear. "Do you like him?"

"Yes, but that is enough talk for now. You must eat and rest. You can tell me what happened later," said Fine Bull.

Lame Bear spent the next few days rebuilding his strength. Word of his recovery was sent to Red Eagle, but his son had requested not to see his father until he was completely strong again. Red Eagle and Fine Bull understood. Lame Bear wanted his homecoming to be something very special.

In the days that followed, Lame Bear told Fine Bull about his adventures in the Flathead valley. The old man's eyes shone with excitement, and he often nodded his approval.

"They almost captured me, Fine Bull. The horses were tired and the Flatheads were closing in on us. I was ready to give up, and then he came and saved us."

"Who came?" asked Fine Bull.

"My spirit helper. He came out of nowhere. He gave the horses strength, and guided them through the storm. We would have been lost in the snow, but he kept us on the trail. I was cold from the river and the sleet. My mind started playing tricks on me. That was when I tied myself onto the horse. The last thing I remember was the angry yells of the Flatheads. They could not see me because it was snowing so hard. They would not follow me into the storm for fear of losing their horses on the treacherous trail." Lame Bear shivered just thinking about it.

When Lame Bear finished his story, both he and the old man sat silently staring into the fire, each lost in his own thoughts. Finally, Fine Bull spoke. "Lame Bear, you have come far. I remember when I saw you sitting by the riverbank last spring. You were weak, both in your body and in your heart. Now your body is strong and your heart is full of courage. You are ready to take the way that will make you a great warrior."

Lame Bear smiled as he remembered. "I had the heart of a rabbit then. But that person is a stranger to me now. I lost him somewhere on my journey to the high places."

"The high places?" asked Fine Bull.

"Yes. The Earth Powers have taken my spirit from the depths of the valley of darkness to the high places, where only the eagles and mountain sheep dare to go. They have given me a vision of something far greater than myself. I am no longer afraid," he said.

"This is good," replied Fine Bull.

"I am ready to return to my father's lodge now," said Lame Bear.

Together, the boy and the old man walked out to where the horses were grazing. Lame Bear whistled to War Chief. The Medicine Hat stallion raised his head and neighed a joyous greeting. Lame Bear left Fine Bull and walked to his horse. The two exchanged affectionate greetings. Then, grabbing a hank of mane, he swung gracefully up on War Chief's back. Sitting straight and proud, Lame Bear rode the stallion through the village to his father's lodge. Red Eagle heard the approaching horse. He lifted the entrance flap and stepped outside. Lame Bear dismounted and went to Red Eagle. The hearts of father and son were full.

Lame Bear and his father clasped wrists and looked into each other's eyes. Red Eagle spoke slowly. "My son, you have brought honor to my lodge. Not only did you win the heart of the Medicine Hat stallion, but you dishonored the mighty warriors of the Flathead nation by stealing him away from them. Lame Bear is no longer a fitting name for you. I think some day you will become a great warrior with many horses in your herd. Tonight there will be a celebration to honor my son, and give you a new name—Many Horses."

War Chief nudged Lame Bear playfully. The boy turned and hugged the stallion's neck, tears brimming in his eyes. "Not only have I brought honor to my father's lodge, but in my quest for courage, I found you, War Chief, my friend."

About the Author

Stormy Rodolph was raised on a horse and cattle ranch south of Livingston, Montana. After graduating from the University of Montana, she taught high school English in the small logging community of Darby, nestled in the Bitterroot Valley. It was there that her vision of writing *Quest for Courage* began.